ACCLAIM FOR *PRISM*

"To me a chainsaw is a highly technical machine, but Austin Bay's prose serves up hi-tech suspense in this fast and futuristic novel, which will keep those of us who are normally satisfied with less on the edge of our BarcaLoungers right up to the last page."

—Tony Hillerman

"Austin Bay has created a New Age assassin who has extraordinary inside knowledge—political, military, economic—covering the complexities of our violent and computerized age. Surely Dashiell Hammett, if alive today, would write as Bay writes—incisive, no-nonsense prose as swift as an assassin's bullet."

—Norman Sherry
Author of *The Life of Graham Greene*

"*Prism* does a brilliant job of combining a post–Cold War spy novel with the cutting edge in near-term science fiction, and it's one of the few Washington 'insider' books I've read that comes close enough to real political personalities to be interesting without copying the personality of some real-World political figures."

—Dr. Tony Cordesman
ABC News military expert
and professor at Georgetown University

Books by Austin Bay

Fiction
The Coyote Cried Twice
Prism

Nonfiction
A Quick and Dirty Guide to War
From Shield to Storm

PRISM

A NOVEL

Austin Bay

HarperPaperbacks
A Division of HarperCollins*Publishers*

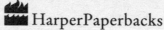
HarperPaperbacks
A Division of HarperCollinsPublishers
10 East 53rd Street, New York, N.Y. 10022-5299

Copyright © 1996 by Austin Bay
All rights reserved. No part of this book may be used or
reproduced in any manner whatsoever without written
permission of the publisher, except in the case of brief
quotations embodied in critical articles and reviews.
For information address HarperCollinsPublishers,
10 East 53rd Street, New York, N.Y. 10022-5299.

ISBN 0-06-109597-4

HarperCollins®, 📖 ®, and HarperPaperbacks™ are trademarks
of HarperCollinsPublishers, Inc.

The hardcover edition of this book was published in 1996 by
HarperCollinsPublishers Inc.

First HarperPaperbacks printing: July 1997

Cover illustration by Corsillo/Manzone

Printed in the United States of America

❖ 10 9 8 7 6 5 4 3 2 1

*This novel is for Annabelle and Christiana,
my daughters, who finally convinced
their slow-to-get-it dad (after two-dozen
runs and reruns of their Disney Sleeping
Beauty video) that Maleficent is indeed a
cool character, and that an evil sorceress
with a conspiratorial vision of history and
a control freak agenda deserves a less
feudal, but equally central,
fictional life.*

Science had taken the ordinary man unawares. Too late now to talk of new world orders. His destruction was imminent.

Eric Ambler, *The Dark Frontier*, 1936

Every time a victim dies it's a small defeat for tyranny.

P. D. James, *The Children of Men*, 1993

One

The phone I refuse to answer buzzed its special buzz. Startled, I looked up from the stack of bills littering my rolltop desk. If there had been a mirror I am certain I would have seen a frightened man in the reflection. You can only hide so much so long.

The telecommunicator code phone made its noise again. It was one of those moments when you simply decide.

I tapped the "Wait" code into the telecommunicator's computer pad. I had no inkling, no sense of mental pressure. So I stood up, went into the closet, opened the wall safe, and ripped the top sheet from the code response pad. I had not used the pad since August 2, 1990, the day Saddam invaded Kuwait and the Persian Gulf War began. I had told myself I would never respond again. But, as if in a dream, here I was.

I shut the safe, went back to the phone, and punched the activation sequence and the cipher into the computer's code-decode system. The light on the phone changed from red to green, indicating my receiver and transmitter had entered the secure mode. At that point, when all the high technology is working and all of the codes and security devices have tapped, policed, and sanctioned one another, the system signals the satellite and says, okay, send what you hope will stay a secret.

The sender replied.

My code phone apparatus received the sender's transmission. The transmission was a burst transmission. Don't let the technobabble and high-tech jargon put you off. The high tech exists because those who have power have to have secrets. Burst transmission gadgetry, like the jargon, like the entire cloak of silicon circuits, smart weapons, and calculated deceit, helps the powerful keep their secrets, conceal the greed, and disguise the ugliness.

My decode receiver (in a quick eternity) expanded the sender's reply.

The reply surprised me.

Okay, her reply stunned me. I was shocked, frightened, and disturbed. The sender was Chatterley, and I hadn't had the slightest sense of anticipation, of her "most able" mental pressure, of probing on her part. So Chatt was indeed in charge, in charge of practically everything.

"You can't say no this time, Wes," she said. "I won't let you."

"You do have that kind of power, Chatt."

"Don't you goddamn assume anything," she snapped. Then she instantly flattened her splinter of anger and political uncool with the usual starch of instruction. "Wesley . . . Wes, for just this once keep your mouth shut and your mind open and don't assume anything. Can you? We've no leeway in this one. Do you follow me? My God, I can't cover for another one of your less than *charming* episodes."

Charming—perfect the way she spiked that word, spoken so bone-china smooth, no nicks, no chinks, no scorch marks on the glaze.

So I kept my mouth shut and let her talk on. With burst transmission gadgetry carrying the traffic I had time to think, to think for myself, to anticipate, to sense a probe. The burst transmission process works like this: a sentence that takes the sender four seconds to speak, instead of being instantly transmitted, is digitally recorded by a computer and at the punch of a button scrambled in code and shrunk into a computer file. The shrunken file is then transmitted in a six-millisecond burst of radio energy. Instead of taking four seconds to transmit (which gives an adept electronic enemy time to find your frequencies and intercept your message), you're only transmitting for six thousandths of a second. The receiver's system picks up the short signal and the reception computer quickly expands and decrypts the recorded message. You hear a replay in real time of the sender's voice. A conversation on a scramble and burst system takes a little longer than one using a simple voice scrambler or straight phone line, but electronic interception is very unlikely. You get the sense that scramble and burst creates a rhythm, a tight communication discipline. In a give-and-take conversation you have to pause. Your sentences become sharp and complete.

And Chatterley's speech was sharp, complete, well devised. So was the operation. The operation she detailed fit within national security parameters, national security being jargon for making sure those with power in the United States get to keep it without challenge. Of course, what she had to say was designed to make sense to me. It was designed to appeal to me. For the moment I was the only constituency Chatterley cared about, my hardened disbelief the only defense she chose to shatter. Chatt outlined the problem Coleman O. Mosley posed. "A power hungry magnate with ten billion dollars and international media exposure is a pertinent security risk," she said in her most terse, clipped style. Then she said a few more things about Mosley. They were calculated comments. And she must have sensed I wanted to believe her, to accept her deceit, for as she finished her comments she studiously avoided the usual Shop cheerleading claptrap about the process of Destruction and Incorporation, that way of the world, of history, and the way America and The Shop developed superior, surefire methods for controlling the process of change. I didn't need to hear that. Chatt knew I did not want to hear that. But I listened to her finish. I realized I was deciding. I was simultaneously accepting her deceit and getting very angry— very angry with her. Chatt knew all of my buttons, the ones to push, the ones to avoid.

My verbal and mental silence must have convinced her I was hooked.

So Chatterley made her own dig. She always has to make her own dig, to let me know that she not only knows what makes me tick but that she has an important part of me, that there are buttons, psychoneurological alleys she does not fear. She laughed her brilliant, seductive laugh. "We love your brains,

Wes, but what Max and I really need are the sex appeal and brawn."

I took a deep breath. The burst transmission code-decode cycle gives you time to breathe like that. "That's what you need? Then the answer is no, you bitch," I said.

My curse bounced off the satellite.

Her reply arrived. Her reply was brighter laughter. Even the digital reconstruction of her laugh managed to capture Chatt's Ivy League arrogance, the radiance, the firm consciousness that she can place, enter, and direct. For a moment I could see her face, dazzling in my mind, the bright hard eyes in the lovely round face.

"Oh ho. *You* can't say no, Wes. Not right now you can't. We know your charming little rebellion's over, don't we? You need money, baby."

I stared at my desk. Chatt and Max (the Max she refers to when she needs to) never give me room to hide. The Shop's computers and psychiatrists know everything about me, everything that can be probed and digitized. My neurons, my life, can be displayed on a wall by an overhead projector.

"Hey—you need cash, don't you," she said again.

I knew I had been researched, very recently.

At that moment I looked up. I had made a mistake. I had not locked my office door. Once again, without any sensation, my daughter seemed to know. The door cracked open and Courtney peered into my office. When her long red hair falls on her shoulders she looks like her mother once looked. I mouthed, silently: "Five minutes, dear." I held up my hand and spread five fingers. Then I formed my fingers and made a motion, one of our scrambled hand sign codes. Courtney nodded. "Okay, Daddy, I'll be sensible and G-O," she mouthed. My twelve-year-old is, like me, a quiet and discreet person.

The door clicked closed as Courtney left.

"Wes?" Chatt asked snappishly. "Wes?"

"Okay. You're right. I need money. Who's been watching me?"

"Fazzari. He's kept himself cloaked, I hope?"

"Yes . . . I need to raise an issue. If I sign on, Chatterley, who takes care of my kid?"

Her laugh again, so damn certain a laugh. "Wow. The macho hunk needs day care?"

"What do you know of the life of a single parent," I shot back.

I waited for my message to reach the satellite, for her system to expand it, for Chatt to hear my words, for the words to resonate in her mind. I waited for her to goddamn think. As I said, she knew my buttons. I trusted a genius like Chatt would know what wall she had just struck. She has memorized my psychological profile. She can enter.

"I'm sorry," Chatt replied.

When I dream at night I dream of Jessica. Chatt knows this. In my dreams Jessica is smiling and she is very much alive. In these apparitions Jessica can hear, she hears Courtney crying, even when her back is turned she hears my words. Jessica does not sign. Her soft hands remain in the pocket of her blue frock, the paint frock the color of her eyes. Jessica smiles, her lips part and she speaks, her new voice cool and precise, without the unshaped stammer of the deaf. That is the instant I admit I am dreaming something that was not. Chatt and her bastards have analyzed computer simulations of my dreams. I know they would prefer my dreams were simple vicious darkness.

"Wes, your aunt will arrive tomorrow."

"My aunt?"

"Barbara Angleton."

"My aunt? My ass." With a Ph.D. in math from Berkeley and a Ph.D. in linguistics from Yale, gray-headed Barb had been, until her retirement in November 1989, The Shop's top cryptoanalyst and section counterintelligence director.

"Now, Wes, you just listen. I don't know of anyone more . . . more protective."

"Paranoid, Chatterley. There's no one more paranoid than Barbara."

"Okay, she's paranoid. Will she do?"

I started to say no, nothing will do, not anymore. But instead the soldier inside me said: "You are in command."

"Good—then it's settled. You understand the thrust of this operation. It's observational."

"It's risky as hell, Chatt. Otherwise you wouldn't call me."

"Hey, you're cost effective," she purred. Then she waited.

I am certain, since Chatt knows my mind, she used that moment to probe. Playing all sides at once, aren't you Chatt, I thought. But that's part of Chatt's physical and psychic genius, to be blonde and brunette, to manipulate all the edges, to twist the poetry as well as the substance.

"Six hundred thousand has been placed in your

account in Lugano. That'll cover initial expenses, get you sprinting. The next payment's in three months. A hefty sum, gads of zeros."

"Where will Courtney go?"

"She can stay where she is. You haven't been compromised. Even though she doesn't like the hot weather down there Barb will move in and follow orders. Your pal Fazzari will stay in the area. He always wanted to be a cowboy. . . . Well?"

I said: "All right. I'm on board."

The time passed. It felt like a long time but it wasn't. Satellite relays, shrinking and expanding sentences inside telecommunications computers rigged with a trillion ciphers, still move at the speed of light.

"I'm glad to get you back." Her reply hung there, saying more than it should, until she added with a degree of sass: "No one can just retire anymore, can they, Wes? Quitting's tough, really tough. Don't we all have to learn that? Retire, try to relax, and the next thing you know you wonder how you can go on . . ."

There was a pause. Her voice hardened: "You know you've talents we need to get this country where it has to be. Now, to finish this business. You will find taped to the mailing label on your latest issue of *The Economist* an information chip. Fazzari put it there this afternoon after the mailman passed. Use your code check set. Now. . . . All the operational details I haven't covered, including a full dossier on Mosley, are contained on the chip. Study it. You can relay your plan using your special set at, let's say, nineteen-hundred hours tomorrow. Any other questions?"

"Who do I contact if something goes wrong."

"How wrong?"

"Rotten, Chatt, totally rotten. So rotten I need an immediate and thorough answer."

"Wes . . ." I could almost detect a schoolmarmish cluck. "Wes. You know how difficult it is for me these days. I've an explicit role. *You* must never try and reach me via a Prism contact."

"You have your means, but what if I try—"

"No," Chatt interrupted. She was angry, that quick burning anger. "Dammit, I order you to never contact me via Prism."

"So . . . you're in when you want to be, unlike the rest of us who aren't allowed to quit."

"I have broader responsibilities. I have critical abilities and responsibilities. Critical. And you of all people appreciate that."

"You're sure I do."

"Yes."

"You sound so damn sure, Chatt."

She laughed.

Okay. She was right. She has the great ability. I am a soldier. They know me, physically, clinically, and I am their creature. If I have a soul they know where it is.

Her laugh continued as she said, "You picked up the code phone of your own volition. Don't deny it. Don't even think about denying it."

I did not reply. We both knew the truth, didn't we. We both knew even without a prism.

"I'll contact you tomorrow," Chatt declared. Her voice was terse and so damned precise. A quick eternity came and went. Then, before the cipher light switched off, she said: "Now . . . now go out and do what you've been trained to do."

Two

A gray French aircraft carrier lay at anchor in the blue water of the bay. Overhead one, then two fighter jets banked from the white morning clouds of the Med and began their long landing glide on a bearing aimed at the naval air station east of the city.

The fan inside the dark apartment pushed a slow circle of air toward my chair on the balcony above the courtyard. I stirred a rocky sugar cube into my cup of mint tea and as it dissolved I closed my eyes. There is never a moment when Toulon does not smell of the sea. In every cranny of the port, in every corner and shadow, you are aware of its presence. I could smell the water. I could also smell fish, diesel fuel, and sweat, the human sweat of stevedores, sailors, barmaids, whores.

I opened my eyes and took a sip of the hot mint tea, the mint and sugar mix sweet and potent. I took another hungry sip, emptying the cup. This morning I would push the process, make certain Maarten introduced me to Monsieur Le Pens. From that point on, my credentials and my ability—yes, my ableness, if that is what it took—would have to get me next to Coleman Mosley.

Lifting the warm porcelain pot I reflected, reflected on its hot yet icy shine, then slowly refilled the teacup.

I had given myself two weeks to reestablish the Carey Hawkins identity. The Hawkins identity had been of extraordinary use to The Shop. In 1975 I had enlisted in the French Foreign Legion under the Hawkins alias. I had endured the Legion's basic training and rites of passage. The Legion rites were more harsh and cruel than my previous bouts of basic training, but not so different. Instructors can only go so far with the brutality. I think the drill sergeants realized I was not a man to brutalize. I did well in basic training, despite portraying Hawkins as being left-handed. I volunteered and was selected for parachute school. It was a ruse, of course. I already had over two hundred parachute jumps under my belt and was High Altitude Low Opening (HALO in the jargon) jump qualified in U.S. Special Forces. After completing parachute training I was posted to Corsica with the Foreign Legion's First Battalion. I was quiet and reserved but made certain I had friends. Friends and acquaintances who would remember Hawkins were part of the mission, an essential feature of The Shop's design.

Six months into my tour of duty the fix began to take. I was assigned to Djibouti with a Foreign Legion detachment, where I also made friends, and from there, because of my demonstrated skills as a sniper, I was seconded to a *dragons militaire* assignment in Chad. I spent three months in N'Djamena showing various African soldiers how to hold a rifle, how to adjust a rifle scope, how to obtain a steady sight picture, how to put the bullet where you want it to go. After a little more than a year in the Legion Carey Hawkins disappeared, supposedly on a mission into Burkina Faso. Others said they had heard Hawkins and two other Legionnaires had been sent north to Tibesti and had been killed by tribesmen. I was, of course, brought back to Northern Virginia. What the arrangements with the French were I can surmise. I know I received in 1978 what looked like bona fide discharge papers. There was also a settlement "in lieu of disability pension" for 110,000 French francs. Apparently Carey Hawkins had stepped on a land mine.

I had become Hawkins twice since then, 1980 in Angola and 1982 in Nicaragua. After Nicaragua Hawkins had been placed in very cold storage, for he had a price on his head, to be paid by the KGB. It was not a large bounty, scarcely six figures. The KGB, even at the height of its Cold War authority, never offered much of anything for anyone.

Before leaving for France I had grayed my hair, a glacial sort of gray, and bushed my eyebrows. I affected a slight limp by the usual method, a cotton wad beneath my left arch. Though ambidextrous, I had not exercised my left hand at writing for some time. Hawkins' signature had been tall and narrow, and I had to practice for a couple of hours before it clicked. Getting his handwriting down helped me re-create the man, to become him physically, mentally.

I made all of these mission preparations alone, relying on myself, my own ability. Barbara Angleton, her gray smoker's face melting in the heat, loaded her Mercedes and took Courtney to the beach for a week.

I was gone before they returned. I did leave Courtney
a note. I stuck the note beneath the lock of her
mother's hair and the lock of my hair she keeps in her
bedroom. I told Courtney I loved her, that in this life
she was the only child who mattered. I told the child I
adored her. I told her to keep safe, to remember the
words we kept between us, our signs, our promises. I
wrote that note in longhand, with my right hand, in
my own handwriting.

I finished the cup of mint tea, not leaving a drop. I got
my flight bag and went to the gymnasium.

I had met Maarten at the gymnasium some ten days
prior, two days after arriving in France. He was a no
one suddenly unique. Chatt had concluded Maarten
could get me to Le Pens and not raise suspicions.
Frankly, there are a lot of men like Maarten, in all
respects, and I have met many of them. He is a man
with a bald head, large chest muscles, eyes a haunted
space of brown and gray. He has his African and
Eleventh Parachute Division tattoos. When his head
bends forward his cheeks sag and the wrinkles on his
forehead gain weight. A gold locket on a gold chain
nestles in the gray hair of his chest.

I knew that Maarten noticed me as I entered the
gym and took a towel from the rack. He lifted
weights, then spent twenty minutes punishing a
punching bag, the gold locket shining from sweat. I
did three calisthenic sets, then retired to sit in the
sauna. I took a book with me, a paperback selected

for its cover: a wounded man wearing a burgundy beret and torn camouflage tee firing a black machine pistol at a wall of leafy, cartoon jungle.

There were at least thirty other men in the wet sauna when Maarten came in and took a seat on the bench opposite me. He looked at everyone, then his eyes settled on me. He watched me well. With puffy fingers he pulled a snag from the dangling gold chain and touched the locket.

As I left the sauna for the shower he said to me in French: "Pardon, my friend. But you've left your book." He pointed toward the paperback on the wood ledge of the sauna.

"I finished it," I replied with a smile. "Do you want it? It's a tale of revenge and rather exciting."

He said, "Yes," a hopeful yes, he would like to have the book. Towel over my shoulder, I gave him the book. But now Maarten was staring at the floor. He started to speak, desired to speak—definite sensation of unease, *the sensation,* and I knew Maarten's desire was lost in discomfit. So I thought (only momentarily, for I knew my limits almost as well as Chatterley), I thought, despite my training and the limits of my ableness, what a perfect moment, if I could enter and suggest, if I could enter and place like Chatterley, if only that were my active degree of ableness, *if I could—*

But of course there was no need. Chatterley knew what it would take (conversation, sauna, a book), no need to risk reliance on ability, that special force, no need at all.

Maarten looked at the floor of the sauna and asked me if I was interested in a beer.

We dressed and left the gym. I let him buy me a couple of beers in a spot near the navy depot. I told him my name was Hawkins. I said I was Irish. Yes, I had been in the Legion, how did he know? He said he was named Maarten and once he was from South Africa, before the Legion. His jaw tightened. He said he had grown tired of patrolling the South African bush. By the time I left he had become quiet, sullen.

Three days later I made sure we met again, this time on the boulevard, the one running past the government offices toward the harbor. I insisted on buying him a beer and he suggested dinner, at a special bistro near the docks. I said I was busy but another time, later perhaps? Yes, Maarten my friend, we'll get together later for certain . . .

Today would be that certain later.

I arrived at the gym. Maarten was smashing the bag. His lip curled forward as he struck his blows. Sweat beaded his wrinkling bald head.

When he finished he came over to me.

"Hawkins," he grinned. "You stuck? Still prowling Toulon?"

I said yes.

"Have good luck with the women?"

I said only so-so.

"Now I'm asking—what keeps you hanging about?"

I said we could discuss that.

He slapped my shoulder with a sweating hand. "Shall we visit the bistros this evening?"

"Of course," I replied.

* * *

Maarten picked a chicken bone from between his teeth and nodded. Of course Maarten knew Jack Le Pens. But as far as he knew the fat Frenchman was not recruiting. "It is no longer the same, not with the Russians going to shit," he said. "The Arabs are not looking. With the Nigerians playing regional god the situation in West Africa is not promising for adventurers. Central Africa? Poor starving bastards. Nothing worth doing since copper and coffee prices went fart. And don't believe the lies about Central Asia, friend. The Armenians have come through looking for men with experience, but those impoverished people pay nothing. As we are all aware, glory doesn't buy anything but a body bag." He put the chicken bone down on the edge of his green plastic plate.

I asked about the Iranians.

"The Iranians are insane, Hawkins, completely . . . though I understand they had a man here a few months ago."

I said I guessed I'd missed that ticket.

"Why is that?"

I said I spoke some Farsi, the Iranian lingo. The Iranians seemed to have money and even if they were insane zealots they paid. Of course, I said, if personal desires were known, if our desires mattered, based upon my most recent experience I preferred working for a private client rather than any government, though government was far preferable to fighting for a religion and religion better than nothing.

Maarten took a sip of white wine, a contemplative sip, and looked at me. In the back of the dive a huge black woman began to play a concertina. An Arab girl began to dance in the smoky blue light. She moved with a dreamlike shimmer, hips, shoulders, her curves, and scarf specific lures and appeals, but her dance a dream, a shift in the thickening smoke.

"So," Maarten finally said, "this is what brings you back. You lost a decent job and are at square one with the sorry rest of us." As he shook his head he shrugged, his smile more sympathetic than derisive. "There are a thousand men within twenty kilometers of Toulon ready to seek work. These times, the chaos, one bad day after another, you might think men with skills, with substantial experience especially in Africa, you would think in the chaos men such as ourselves would find a spot. We should find a position. But the financing, poof, gone. We have been dropped, stranded, leftovers on the battlefield." A puffy prizefighter's finger touched the gold chain around his neck, wormed its way around the locket. "Tell me, Carey. You are Irish, Protestant I would guess. No? Catholic? Really . . . have you been to Belfast lately? No? No interest, eh. None at all?" Maarten decided not to explore that question. What answer he imagined I would give seemed to suffice.

Then his lids lowered over his bulbous eyes as he took another sip of wine. "I've inquired about you, checked up with people. I hope you do not mind." His eyelids rose and once more he brushed the gold chain across his chest. Chatt had counted on an investigation by Maarten. Checking into me would be part of the man's routine of subterfuge, his method of survival. Finding out who I was part of his habit, his life process, a bit part in Chatt's larger process.

"Do you remember a man named Meiner from First Parachute?" he asked.

I said no, I did not.

"Oh. Perhaps it was Djibouti. He remembers you, rather clearly. Meiner says you are a quiet fellow and a crack rifle shot . . . very steady."

I said I still did not remember him by name but might by sight.

These remarks played well in the theater of Maarten's mind.

"Meiner says he's wondered what you might've done for paychecks these last few years."

I told him South America. Personal security work. And I would leave it at that.

"Really? Personal security work. A corporation? One of those multinational things? You speak Spanish?"

"Hablo perfecto."

"Salud." Maarten, impressed, raised the wineglass. I raised mine. The wineglass and stem, momentarily, caught and broke the cool smoky light like a gentle, imperfect prism.

That evening Maarten introduced me to Le Pens. The restaurant where I met Le Pens was a much cleaner place than the bistro near the docks. Ceiling fans, the slow blades painted ivory, revolved like stiff flowers. The band had three musicians and the drinks were more expensive. The prostitutes circling the bar were white and Asian girls.

"My good friend Carey Hawkins has a knack for languages," Maarten said to Le Pens. Maarten put his hand on my shoulder, a faint hand with a gentle squeeze. "And he's worked the Americas."

I recognized, sitting in the booth behind Jack Le Pens, Herr Uwe Meiner. He looked exactly like his picture in Chatt's dossier. Chatt's brief had said Meiner worked for Le Pens, moving guns and ammo to Africa. Meiner also scouted talent for Colonel Raymond "Bullet" Garcia, my real objective in Chatt's involved process. Garcia hired muscle for Coleman Mosley.

"Sit down," Le Pens said crisply.

Le Pens appeared to be a fatter, less muscular version of Maarten, his paunch not what one would expect of a former Legion officer. Le Pens' threads were silk and linen, his tie a paisley relic, his blue eyes sharp and bright. After the rites of welcome Le Pens asked Maarten to visit the bar. "I doubt you'll find one your type," Le Pens said with no emotion.

Maarten replied with a shrug. He went to the bar. He snuggled, uncomfortably, between two Asian women. I suppose he ordered beer.

I waited, with caution and discipline. The chubby Le Pens was finishing a plate of rice, sausage, and shrimp. He took his time, knocking the prawns across the green china, sopping with white bread. I watched his eyes. I am certain he was looking for the okay from Meiner, the nod confirming that I was Hawkins. I was—no, amend that—Chatterley was counting on it.

Le Pens finished a greedy bite and smiled. He withdrew a pack of cigarettes, Gitanes, and lit one, wiping the match in the air, then tossing it on the floor. "So. You've done some personal security work in South America and you speak Spanish. Who'd you soldier for?"

I said I would rather not say. Le Pens responded gruffly and said if we were going to get anywhere I would have to. So I gave the German's name.

I didn't have to spell it out.

Jack Le Pens' jaw dropped. "You're kidding—that fucking Nazi!? You guarded a goddamn *Reichsführer*?"

I glared at him. Le Pens' reaction, of course, had been exactly what Chatt had thought it would be when she began to create this operation. I am certain that Chatt, to a degree, had put herself inside Le Pens' head and inside Mosley's as well.

Le Pens must have developed a hellacious itch in his ear. He scratched his left lobe furiously, the smoke from the cigarette curling around his head like the hot arm of a ghost.

"Whoa," he said. "You aren't kidding."

"No."

"That fucking Nazi? He survived after all, did he?" Le Pens took a long draw on his cigarette, then mashed the smoke into the green china plate. "What happened."

"He finally died."

"Where? How? Sweet blue shit, man."

"Please. This isn't relevant, Monsieur Le Pens."

"No. Not relevant, but goddamn interesting. Extremely interesting." Le Pens signaled for some wine.

I gave him the story Chatterley concocted.

Le Pens could barely contain himself. His hand wiped at the linen edge of the tablecloth, choppily, back and forth over the bread crumbs, a shallow oar in deep water. "Bolivia. Of course. The altiplano and the Andes. If the Incas could retreat into cities of the sun, why not a Nazi? But Mossad, Mr. Hawkins. The Israelis, weren't they on his tail?"

I said, yeah, the Israelis were after him. They had an in absentia. Mossad tried twice to fulfill the execution, but the half dozen security men, including myself, had learned a great deal about countering the Israelis' methods.

"You're good at thwarting the Jews?"

I let his remark stand unchallenged.

"And you speak Spanish?"

I nodded.

"And German?"

"Ich kann deutsch."

After Le Pens raised his hand and crooked a finger, Uwe Meiner joined us.

"Nothing hot's going on these days, Hawkins," Le Pens said. "But my associate here is helping with special security services. Rock-and-roll music stars, I think . . . well, he'll explain."

Meiner, still thin and lithe, sat down next to me. His eyes, like gray mirrors in his narrow face, focused on me. At that moment I had a sensation, an inkling, a weak one, primitive and flimsy, unintentional and opaque, one that could never be emphasized and focused in the highest quality, most absorbing prism, much less used as a calculated probe. I startled, naturally I would startle at confronting unexpected ability, even primitive ability, but I was more intrigued than concerned, for it took no effort or arrogance on my part to follow orders and cloak, to block it out and control.

Finally, Uwe Meiner said: "C'mon . . . do you remember me now?"

" . . . Maybe . . . hell, I don't know."

He pursed his lips and looked at Le Pens. His look was an I-told-you-so.

"We were in First Parachute together. For three, four months."

"No," I lied. "I'm sorry, I don't remember."

"You were in Second Company, weren't you. And your nickname was 'Irish.'"

"Yeah . . ."

Meiner smiled again.

"Don't be nervous, Hawkins. Uwe remembers everyone," Le Pens said, his face reddening. He sensed, clearly sensed, that I was a man who would bring them a finder's fee from Garcia and Mosley. "Uwe has a photographic memory for people's faces and names. And dates as well. Dazzling ability, isn't it, a photographic memory? Must have peculiar neurons, eh, Hawkins? We think his son's inherited the trait. Aw, don't deny it, Meiner, we know the boy has a certain genius." Le Pens leaned, eagerly, across the table. "Useful skill, huh? Damn big time useful skill. We require security as well as flexibility in our line of work. Uwe, with his mind, is a bit like a computer, with the bonus that he can't be tapped, eh? Uwe also shoots better than most computers, at least the ones I've seen. Drinks more, too." Le Pens winked at Meiner.

I forced a smile. Candy ass photographic memory—weak, primitive, a step from unable, a bare step from the usual unable darkness. Had Chatt known? Would she be amused? I decided—as if *I* could decide—yes, Chatterley would indeed be amused.

Three

It took two days, then Mosley's money began to show along the edges and in the mechanism of the hiring process.

Le Pens gave me a coach ticket to Zurich. I was to go to an address in Zurich where I would be fingerprinted and photographed. A blood sample would also be taken. "You understand," Le Pens grinned. "After all, you were recommended by Maarten."

I told Le Pens I understood.

I was to wait in a hotel in Zurich until called. I was to eat my meals at the hotel. At that point, Meiner confided, if I passed everything, if I got through the bullshit, I would be sent to Paris. Of course all of my expenses would be paid and even if I was not hired I would receive twenty-five hundred Swiss francs. I was not to inquire at all as to who was hiring.

"His record label is very nervous," Le Pens lied.

I knew Coleman Mosley liked the feel of subterfuge, of the supposedly macho life of mercenaries, spies, the CIA, of commando dash and daring. You would have thought his experience as a Wall Street investment banker or his years in global oil exploration would have cured that illness, the sobering experience of work and sweat erasing the boyish appeal of bloody killers, his billions of dollars far more satisfactory than a lousy green beret. But some men, particularly those who see themselves as ending up too short or too small, or those who never served in uniform themselves, these pocket Napoleons go to great and all-too-obvious lengths to compensate for the physical inches and gut experience they lack. You don't need Chatt and her neural teams to document that psychological warp in Mosley. Despite never having served in any military (he was too busy with education, with preparing to make money), Mosley ran his corporations as if they were high-tech combat divisions. His corporate business plans were computerized conflict simulations, updated at thirty-minute intervals. His foreign trade representatives were skilled intelligence operatives. Coleman Mosley's demand for information—useful information, which meant critical information, which became *manipulative* information—was exceeded only by his paranoia and megalomania. Mosley hired private eyes on the drop of a hint. One of Chatt's dossiers proved that Coleman Oswald Mosley had wiretapped his own cancer-ridden mother.

I took the ticket and went to Zurich. I gave blood and urine. I waited another two days, until the phone call came. Twenty-five hundred Swiss francs were waiting at the desk, as well as a ticket to Paris.

I napped on the cab ride in from the airport and awoke as the cab left the A-1 at the Péripherique. I looked at the sidewalks, the sycamore trees along the boulevards, the red and yellow awnings of the shops and cafes, the passing buildings of textured gray stone. That is the stone of Paris.

The cab stopped on rue Castiglione, close enough for my purposes. I walked southeast toward the Cathédral St. Roches, and at the corner of rue St. Honoré and rue St. Roches I turned north onto St. Roches. I found the address: 33 rue St. Roches, Restaurant L'Haut-il, the dive as described in my instructions.

Inside the cramped little restaurant I sat down. My instructions reeked of Mosley's paranoia, of his enchantment with CIA con artists. I was to wait five minutes, so Bullet Garcia could size me up and make certain I had not been tailed.

The wine posters tacked to the white plaster walls and pinned above the restaurant's bay window were, by French standards, utter scandal: they advertised American wines, Napa Valley, California, and Yamhill County, Oregon. A more ancient commercial exploitation: to the right of the bay window a small mirror hung from a square-peg nail, the red letters of the name LUCKY STRIKES fading with the mirror's silver.

I heard a woman in the back humming, humming aimlessly. There was a porthole cut in the wall between the kitchen and the small dining area. I saw a large red apron over a stout chest. She peeked around the corner from the kitchen. Yes, a huge woman. She disappeared. She reappeared carrying a broom. She was a fat, huge woman and she continued to hum as she swept.

"Bon," she said. Not good day, just good. She

continued to sweep. She swept a film of dust out the front door, then went back into the kitchen.

I waited five minutes, per the cinematic instructions, then went to the bathroom. I made use of it, a French porcelain slit with a pull chain.

I came back out and sat down. A black girl with very thin lips, with Somali or Ethiopian features, sat at the table near the doorway. A sheaf of gold bracelets circled her right arm. Her head angled away from me. She had long hair drawn back into a bun, making her lean face look even thinner, her high cheekbones like church rafters. She stared out the window, stared at the backstreet as if her Paris were a prison colony, her long legs slinking from the black leather miniskirt, the dressy black leather jacket sleek and shiny as her skin.

The stare at Paris ended. Her head moved, the movement freezing hard for an awkward instant as she saw her own reflection in the Lucky Strikes mirror on the wall.

Then her face rotated toward mine. The distant eyes, widened by the hot splash of violet eye makeup, were simultaneously elegant and stunning. No doubt she was a model or a mistress or maybe someone on the U.N. payroll signed up as a spokeswoman for African famine relief work. No doubt she worked for Mosley.

I had to stop myself. I had many doubts about her and no sensations. It appeared, given the queer Zen startle that registered when she caught her own face among the red letters of Lucky Strike, this looker might have some doubts about herself.

I glanced at my watch and signaled the old woman. I would start the witless routine.

"A glass of the Frog's Leap," I said.

"Certainly," the old woman replied.

The big woman returned with a previously opened bottle and a wineglass. The label on the bottle read STAG'S LEAP. "This is not Frog's Leap, but I am sure it is what you meant," the woman said with a jolly chuckle. "Try it. Not too shabby for American. Stag's Leap from California. You drink it, eh? I'll get you some onion soup." The old woman spun a mouthful of wine in the glass, then toddled off, leaving the bottle on the table.

I picked up the glass, sniffed, then gazed at the wine. I waited.

"They serve the wine you gotta have over in the cathedral," the looker said. Her voice was nicely chilled, her French excellent. She had on the sunglasses now, designer chrome, and was standing near the table. As she leaned toward me I noticed the thin stitch of ritual scar, an intricate fret of pocked, braided flesh circling her neck. "What you must have. Fifth row from the rear," she said. "The confessional. Wait one minute. Don't follow me . . . don't."

She walked out, slender, nervy.

I took a sip of the American wine, put three francs in change on the table, waited one minute, then left.

As I entered the Cathédral St. Roches I crossed myself. My Baptist grandmother hated Catholics. I am not a Catholic but Carey Hawkins is. A man with Mosley's assets and paranoia watches for such slips.

I marched to the fifth row from the rear. The curtain on the confessional was drawn. The entrance to the priest's box was closed. I went into the confessional, sat down, and, per instructions, drew the curtain.

"You are serving Frog's Leap," I said. The words sounded absurd but I did not feel absurd. I would bet, however, Colonel Raymond "Bullet" Garcia did.

The moment of silence seemed reflective. I stared at the dark gauze. I could almost make out the face.

"Okay . . . you have spoken to no one about our arrangement," Garcia began.

I said no, I had spoken to no one.

"We have checked your credentials."

I remained silent.

"You really worked security for that big-time Nazi? A fucking *Reichsführer*?"

"Yes."

"And you've talked to no one about it? Not some reporter?"

"I exercise discretion."

"You sure as hell do."

Then Garcia switched to Spanish. He asked me if I had ever been to Panama or Costa Rica or Nicaragua. I replied in Spanish and said yes, I had been to all three countries but was by no means an expert in the region. He said I spoke excellent Spanish and he detected, correctly, a Mexican accent. I said one of the men I worked with in South America had been Mexican.

"Really? What was his name."

"Portales."

"And where is Portales these days?"

"I don't know. We were asked to leave Bolivia. We were dispersed quickly, I should say."

He asked me what I knew of U.S. politics. I said I

watched CNN. We had a satellite dish in Bolivia and watched a lot of U.S. sports shows. Portales was a Chicago Cubs fan. Garcia asked what my political beliefs were. I said if I were back in Northern Ireland I might have some political beliefs. He asked what I meant by that. I said what I meant was that I was careful. I was a soldier, a professional soldier.

He was quiet for a moment, then said I needed to give him some straight answers. It might be important in this job. What did I think of, say, the Irish Republican Army? Not much, I said. My only surviving sibling, a sister, had been blown up by an IRA bomb. Didn't matter that she and I were Irish Catholic. I said he could check that fact out. He replied that they already had. But tell me a little more about what you think, Hawkins, he insisted. I said, all right, I'd try. I said that while I was apolitical, in my gut I had always been a Laborite. There can be no just politics without populism. "But what I have come to conclude is that the world needs strong leaders. Men who can make hard decisions and then implement them. Men who will act for the good of the people. There is so much poverty."

Then Garcia said, in English: "What do you think of America's current leaders."

"Randall Duncan and what's the other fellow's name, the environmentalist freak, Alan Masterson?"

"Yes."

I said what Chatt had told me to say. "Not much. President Duncan's a bumbler. He's confused. But so was that Republican in there before him."

"President Grover Renwick."

"Yes."

"Didn't like Renwick, huh."

I said what Chatt had told me to say: "Renwick struck me as your typical rich guy. Inherited cash. Detached. A snitty guy never getting the picture. Lots of options for the rich and zero for the poor. He shows you why everyone should be born without money. I'm not against making money, you understand. But people if they're going to run things should know what it's like not to have it."

Garcia chuckled. I think he must have been leaning forward, right next to the confessional screen. I saw the outline of his face.

Then I added, though Chatt had not told me to say this: "The only one in the whole American government with guts and brains is Duncan's first lady. She did a good job when she was lieutenant governor in Virginia, I hear."

Garcia's chuckle turned into a laugh. "Now, Hawkins, you were making sense up until that point. That's one power-hungry, driven bitch. Carolyn Duncan intends to be president. That's not smoke."

I shrugged. I said it because I meant it: "There's a certain appeal about her."

"What do you mean?" He was taken by surprise.

"I mean, she's a woman, she has a certain sensuality. A striking intellect."

Garcia's laugh became a snort. "You think Carolyn Duncan's sexy? The first lady? Jeez, man, you've spent too much time on that Nazi mountain in Bolivia. Intelligence doesn't do anything for the tits, you know what I mean? She hear you say something like you think she's sexy and she'll hunt your *huevos*, buddy. Why the hell do you think Randy Duncan runs around on her? Can't sleep with a tigress like that."

"I thought they had a kid."

"Their boy? Hardin Duncan? I wouldn't be surprised if the kid was someone else's. I mean that. The young man's a nerd. Electronics whiz. The kind of techno-boy she can totally command and control."

"Well. What the hell do I know."

"Aw, you can't know anything about them. Most Americans really don't. I get all this inside stuff from my pals in the Secret Service. Man, the Duncan White House. A real freak shop . . . okay. Any opinions about anyone else?"

"Like what do you mean."

"Say that guy Ted Rebukman on CNN? The *Crossfire* guy? The one who ran against Renwick from the right."

I said what Chatt had told me to say: "I've seen him. We watched that sometimes in Bolivia. He's a bore."

"What about the religious right."

"Who are they."

Garcia gave me a few names.

I shrugged. "I don't know. I don't mean this as a joke. There were some things we could get on the satellite that we didn't watch. Why are you asking me these questions."

"I'm curious. And it's important."

Then I said, exactly as Chatt had suggested: "I guess there's also that bald fellow. You know, with the red mustache."

I heard Garcia draw a breath.

"I think he's okay," I continued. "In Bolivia we used to watch him on Larry King."

"You did, huh."

"Yeah. You know the fellow I'm talking about, the billionaire? Wasn't he in the Marines?"

"Uh . . . yes. Yeah, he was in the Marines."

"I understand that kind of man."

"What kind of man."

"A man with guts."

"Right. Anything else."

I said, according to Chatt's script: "Look, I don't know what you're after. I feel very stupid. I don't know much about these things. You know my background. You have to take it for what it is. I'm not a politician."

I heard Garcia draw another deep breath. I heard a tap-tap sound. Garcia was tapping the wooden side of the confessional. He was nervous. He was making up his mind.

When he had made up his mind he said: "Okay, Hawkins. My name's Ray Garcia. I handle European security work for a special client. A big client. I don't have a final say in this hiring, but what I think goes a long way with the Employer. He's usually hired his people from U.S. Special Forces, that's my background, or Marines. Occasionally British SAS. But the Employer is looking for other people. He intends to expand the security business. Go global with the security business. When I heard about you from Le Pens I called the Employer and he said check you out. He didn't believe the Nazi shit. But it checked."

I said it better have checked.

Then Garcia gave me the address of a hotel. He told me to go to a room and wait. The room he said would be unlocked. He told me I would be there for the afternoon. If I wanted anything get room service.

Then Garcia told me to leave the confessional first. He would follow. And yeah, don't laugh, Garcia said, but he had to admit that he was wearing a clerical collar, white but loose. The Employer went in for close details like that, Garcia said. Real close details.

I left the cathedral and went to the designated hotel off rue St. Honoré. The vines and wrought iron of the hotel's facade, the pale gray eyes of the old concierge, the sensual, frayed creak of the stairs made the place the kind of quaint Parisian hostel romantics see in dreams, in dreams of desire. I walked up to the room. It was a small room with a single bed and a single chair. A sweet bouquet of fresh violets stood on the lamp table beside the single bed. I liked that touch. The flowers tricked the eye, the nick of color catching the first glance long enough to muddle then disguise the room's cheap grime and austerity.

I sat down in the straight-back chair and made a show of sitting. No doubt the room was bugged and I was being filmed, for there was the pressure of a camera lens, a pressure I sensed, on my skin, in my awareness.

To avoid the pressure—to escape that creeping sensation of the camera lens, curiously like a primitive ableness focused and reinforced through a prism—I cloaked. I cloaked my ability, to protect it. I followed orders, I swear it. Don't ever abuse individual ableness, most-able Chatterley had emphasized. "And this operation, Wes," Chatt had said, "of all operations, focus on your telekinetics. Avoid your goddamned will to do what you're not able to do." Sure thing, Chatt,

I'd replied, you bet, I know I'm nothing but a weapon.
And I did know, I recognized my limits, my parameters. So I followed orders. When I felt that hidden lens
sensation (hard sensation, cold sensation), I did it right
and cloaked tight. Cloaking masks ability, limits
chance connections, blunts unfocused psychic probes,
shields your psychic vigor. But—like the room's out of
whack and spiked, in and out, no lens this potent,
man, a glass wall of ice, compressing ice, an old
experiment, my secret will to—

No, not an attack, no snazzy convulsions, no
ridiculous TV explosions. I blinked, gripped the hotel
chair, *aware of dark burn*. I felt it. *Good shatter*—
my cloak totally crashed, splintered into bizarre frags.
Dark mirrors. I sat in the hotel chair, amazed. *The
fractures*. Able pulses, a hyper-prism revolved,
spread is-was-is, time blending, now-then-now
escaped the fragged cloak, the room, local points in
four dimensions. Ableness swapped energies along
dark edges, *burning through facets*, as Chatterley
says it can't ever burn without selecting guidance and
discipline. So, dammit, I applied brutal discipline.
When ableness burns Chatterley angers, and she
greatly angers. But discipline flopped, the cloak
attempt ripped into chaos, chasm, hallway—*Alert*—
where I tried to probe, now cruising free with it, probing like past experiments with Jessica, but the
surprising specifics right *here* like they'd never been
here for me. And as I worked the psychic energy
burn—that instant—I was able as I'd never been. I
shaped it with more-able cool as my training kicked
in—for I was aware of someone concerned with specific orders, someone concerned with the specific

detail of two thousand francs worth of enticement, a guy concerned with sensual body and appeal now hiking up the hotel staircase, traipsing down the hallway . . .

I heard a knock at the door. The handle turned. Yeah, I felt in control. The change was over, done with. Training kicked in hard as the burn dissolved. Okay, time to soldier. I knew Chatt's plan. The door handle stopped. Time to show it, I decided, let the camera know. I reached down to my calf and pulled the throwing knife from its sheath. It was an extruded plastic knife, hard as carbon steel, but able to elude metal detectors. I held the blade up so the camera could see it—then palmed the knife.

A young man cracked the door, then stepped into the room. He had blond hair and large blue eyes. He wore a pec-tight black shirt and blue jeans. A shining silver band wrapped his left wrist. He was clean-cut, the energized replica of a committed Peace Corps volunteer, if you ignored the metal on his wrist and the lazy reptile in his eyes. "Oh, pardon me," he said in French. "I must have the wrong room."

"That's all right," I replied. Yeah, discipline had kicked in, good control. I kept the knife hidden.

He flashed a charming smile and waited a moment. "My name is Tomas," he said with a lot of teeth.

"You have the wrong room, Tomas."

"I do."

"Yes."

"Yes, I certainly do," he replied. He flashed the charming smile once more.

He left. I returned the knife to its no-longer-secret

sheath. I went and poured myself a glass of mineral water.

Twenty minutes later the next temptation. "Pardon, monsieur." She was attractive, the chambermaid, a calculated stunner. She had her black hair back in a taut bun, jet black hair to crush with your fingers. Her work outfit was black, black and tight enough to catch the shape and bounce of her breasts. Thank heavens there was no doily lace—that would have been a touch too Hollywood.

She remade the perfectly made bed, red finger-nails smoothing the ice white pillow.

I figured her for a high-priced hooker hired for something afternoonish and bizarre.

Her white knee touched, grazed the edge of the bed.

When I stood up she did a vicious pirouette and faced me, the smile as instant and professional as they come, the glint in her eyes and the swell of her breasts the practiced remnants of allure.

"Don't let me bother you. I'm just getting another glass of water." I poured the Vichy.

Who knows what she thought, and I did not try for an inkling, not even a sensation. A hooker in Paris has seen every kind of man there is, the aggressive, the reluctant, the sick, the icy, the puzzling, perhaps even the able. The woman put two fingers on her lips. One of the fingers had a bend in it, the crook a bro-ken digit gets when left unset. Whatever the woman thought she thought. The glint in her eyes became the usual what-the-hell. She turned, gave the bed cover a tug, then left. She did have very long legs and a nice perky ass, the kind that lifts up even if she isn't wearing high heels.

Waiting: A half hour passed, a disciplined half hour. That change—come and gone. Chatt's plan was on track. I thumbed a copy of *Le Figaro* that I found in a niche above the toilet, and I was briefly intrigued with the newspaper's short review of a post–Cold War novel that mimed Dante's *Inferno*—you know the grind, a descent into contemporary hell—and was momentarily engaged by a crisply written editorial examining French weapons sales in Rwanda, Burundi, and Zaire. Tossing the newspaper aside, I opened my airline bag and pulled out a paperback, this one with blond-haired, white-winged angels dancing on the cover. Another hour elapsed, this time period one with less discipline, but just as my mind began to stray, to explore that ableness which had so surprised me and taken my discipline unawares, the room phone rang.

It was Bullet Garcia on the line: "Be downstairs in ten minutes. Don't say anything to the concierge, don't even tip her. A cab will take you to the airport."

"De Gaulle?"

"No, it's a private airport about fifty kilometers west of Paris."

"So I passed both the blood and hormones tests?" I asked without a trace of emotion.

Garcia snickered.

Four

The aircraft waiting at the "free-trade zone airport" west of Paris was a brand-new Cessna Citation X with a U.S. N-series ID number. The intercontinental business jet had a six-seat configuration instead of the usual eight, a large fold-up table replacing the two missing passenger seats. Chatt's info chip had prepared me for the railroad: two loops of micro-gauge toy train tracks formed a figure eight on the table's Formica top. Even aloft Coleman Mosley had to have his model trains. At his home hacienda in San Antonio Mosley kept a collection of hundreds of model railroad engines and thousands of cars.

Both of the Citation's pilots were ex–Air Force fighter pilots. When Garcia introduced me to "Sam and Dave" neither Sam nor Dave had much to say other than hello. I had read Sam Peters' and David Clay's dossiers, and they were impressive. Both men had Iraqi MiG kills in Operation Desert Storm. Mosley liked hiring a combat record. Coleman Mosley hired people who had already pulled a trigger, who had already crossed that bloody ditch and crossed it with success.

Garcia put me on the airplane and said: "Enjoy the ride. You got it all to yourself, Hawkins."

"Thanks."

"Okay. Good luck with the Employer. He's gonna like you." Garcia stuck his hand out and I shook it.

The Citation refueled in Gander in the area reserved for private jets. I deboarded and strolled around in the cool Canadian afternoon. Five minutes later Pilot Sam tromped out of the aircraft and told me, "Stay close to the plane. We're splitting as soon as it's juiced. If you want fresh coffee, I just ordered some and the trolley'll bring it out." He pointed toward the general aviation shed.

I put my hands in my pockets and wandered toward the tail end of the aircraft. There were a couple of other transcontinental business jets on the tarmac at Gander, a Dassault Falcon 2000 and a Canadair Challenger. From its ID number I recognized the Falcon as another of Mosley's planes, part of an impressive air fleet. According to one of the files Chatt had sent on the info chip, Mosley maintained a stable of forty-three personal prop, jet, and rotary-wing aircraft. Of that private air force a half dozen planes and one chopper were demilitarized combat aircraft, which, according to Chatt, could be remilitarized very quickly. Mosley had a rebuilt B-26K bomber (purchased from the CIA after the Company used it to bomb Cuba), a rebuilt World War II–era P-51 Mustang (on display at his private airport), an F-104 Starfighter (allegedly used for "high-speed research"), a "C" model of the P-3 Orion (an ex-Navy long-range antisubmarine and electronics warfare aircraft, capable of carrying depth charges and anti-ship missiles), a twin-seat F-5 Freedom Fighter fighter-bomber trainer (with all of the combat avionics and weapons "hard points" and a customized enlarged internal fuel tank) and an F-106 Delta Dart (a long-range interceptor jet aircraft, allegedly used for "courier work"). The ex-military helicopter was a re-engined HueyCobra "S" model attack helicopter (on display at his private airport as a "memorial for Vietnam veterans"). Chatt said Mosley was in the process of purchasing two MiG-29 fighters from the Ukraine government. That had been "the former red flag," Chatt had punned, that raised Shop concerns about Mosley's quest for weapons. None of these aircraft are toy trains. They are not micro-gauge replicas of reality, Chatt had said. They are, she had said, getting in her subtle dig, much like you, Wes, such sophisticated weapons. Chatt wanted to discover what the hell else Coleman O. Mosley might try to buy from cash-starved ex-officers in the Ukrainian, Russian, Kazakh, and Belarussian militaries and intelligence services.

I had no reason to doubt that's what she wanted, did I? The shopping list of a frustrated would-be president with ten billion dollars to spend could be terrifying. Nerve gas, nuclear weapons, biological weapons, advanced lasers, pulse weaponry, micro-robots, and programmed viruses for killing computers, they are available. The fear-mongers on television have flacked them all. Every novel you pick up has someone stealing a nuclear-tipped cruise missile and trying to sell it to Iraq. The tough challenge is to find an able heretic who disputes the techno-catechism and silicon creed, one with discipline. But Chatt was right, you didn't have to have ability, you didn't have to exercise peculiar ableness to know this time Chatterley was precisely correct. Mosley was the kind of guy who could turn hype and spin and a few well-placed bullets into a new political reality. Mosley had excellent connections worldwide, in London, Moscow, Delhi, Riyadh, Paris, Mexico City, and inside Iran. Chatt's worst-case scenario had Mosley helping the mullahs in Tehran haul a half dozen nuclear bombs into the States and blackmailing the president. With activated nuclear weapons hidden throughout American hill, dale, cities, and suburbs, the huge U.S. nuclear arsenal and high-technology conventional combat forces would prove to be expensive gadgetry—gadgets with very little practical use.

Of course Chatt and Max weren't going to let that kind of embarrassment occur. Chatt had thought the Iranian scenario improbable, however. She emphasized a more probable scenario: Mosley was after technology that would give his corporations a competitive edge in the dog-eat-dog of the New World Order's economic competition. As freaky and impetuous as Mosley was, he might try to hire everything from psychics to nuclear physicists to Amazon Indians with exotic neurotoxins on their blow darts.

But another Mosley scenario had come to The Shop's attention. Chatt said rumor had it that the Texan was in the market for an assassin. For a gifted assassin.

And that was no longer a probabilistic scenario. In recruiting me Mosley had just hired himself the world's best.

Chatt wanted me to find out why.

Sam and Dave kept the plane steady as I slept on the leg from Gander to San Antonio. I slept, I dreamed of nothing, and I am certain I did not dream of Jessica. No doubt the dreams without content and specificity pleased Chatt. Not dreaming of Jessica might have pleased her more if it had surprised her. But she and Max know that when I am operational I am theirs. When I am operational and disciplined Chatterley has me.

The Citation landed at Mosley's private airport in southern Texas. The private airport has an official name three sentences long. Mosley's savvy public relations company had nicknamed it "The Area."

The Area is a huge base complex primed for the post–Cold War economic struggle. The place is laid out with the connective logic of a microcircuit. The highways, monorail lines, hike and bike paths all move across the plannedscape like perfect corporate flowcharts. Large glass-and-metal skyscrapers (each sprouting a forest of antennas and satellite dishes) line the interstate highway and the private freeway entering the base. High-tech assembling facilities (for nothing is manufactured but everything is assembled) feed huge warehouses. One side of the warehouse abuts a railroad link, another a truck loading dock, another pushes goods onto the palletized-load vehicles that rush toward the jumbo jet air freighters waiting on the landing aprons of the aerodrome.

And green has its place. In each curl of street, in the corridors between buildings, in the open spaces adjacent to the airport, Mosley's Green Police have planted appropriate species. A hectare of poppy red flowers covers the fuel tanks behind the air freighters' flight line. Mosley received a Distinguished Environmentalist Award from Vice President Masterson for that bit of camouflage. Chatt had specifically marked that fact in a file on Masterson. Chatt had put together a large dossier on Masterson—dozens of glossy photos, pages of documents with red ink notes scrawled on the margins. The computer diskette in the dossier had sixteen files covering Masterson's speech patterns and vocal mannerisms. I had not asked her why I needed to know everything about Masterson, why anyone needed that much info on how he talked, and I was given no inkling.

My return to Texas: I smiled as I walked away from the Citation and headed toward the silver Jaguar that Pilot Dave had said Mosley's Security Detachment Two-Zero had sent for me. I had to smile. I made sure it was a smile and not a smirk because I knew I was being monitored and videotaped. The entire base-complex has videocams stuck in the walls, in the conduits, in the branches of the native species. I had to smile because it is funny. I had to go to France to get to Texas, or at least go to France to get inside

Mosley's New World Order base located on soil that at one time fell inside the boundaries of lines on a map some politicians, after a war or two and an Indian genocide, called Texas. In the chaos of the New World Order the boundary lines aren't relevant anymore. The old lines on the old maps won't show you much of anything about who can put what where and keep it there. The only line that will mean much is the bottom line on the corporate report, and that is a line that will be smudged, smeared, covered with a hectare of shrubs and red flowers.

But to go to Toulon to get to San Antonio? That's what this nightmarish task demanded. Give her credit. Chatt had examined the angles when she created her plan.

We had discussed the operation and my evaluation of her plan on the telecommunicator the day after she had called me and I had answered. I was ready. The phone buzzed at precisely 1900 hours and her attitude was all business. Given her plan's parameters I sketched out what I thought I could do. Then I told her, Yeah, Toulon to get to San Antone is brilliant, Chatt. Your scenarios are compelling. You must have had Net Assessments Section working night and day for a month.

I flattered her. Flattery is one of her buttons she will let me push.

Well, she said, most covert operations directed at a specific country are not run from inside the target country. That is an operational security caution. But it seems to be a common fact of Americana, doesn't it, Wes, that in certain lines of work if you want to come back home you must go away. In certain lines of work authenticity is enhanced if you appear to come out of somewhere else. For some reason escaping logic but comprehensible as psychology and poetry, Chatt said, the hired gunslinger from out of town is always more persuasive than the local deputy. Lies and legend do things for your rep that daily exposure to fact cannot.

Chatt then argued that the same thing applies to politicians. And it dovetails with this operation, Wes. Look at the nosedive in popularity President Randall Duncan took after he went into office and started flailing around, nominating ex–Playboy Bunnies to cabinet positions, looking like a bumbler.

Yes, that happened, I admitted. But Chatt, Duncan's mess-ups surprise me, I said. They surprise me very much. In fact the mess-ups make zero sense. Chatt, why is he being allowed to—

But Chatterley cut me off with a knife blade for a voice. That isn't your concern, Wes, she said, not at all your concern.

But I ignored the knife and didn't stop. Chatt, I said, given your most-ableness you'd think—

No, she snapped, you have no need to know, no need to know, no requirement to understand anything beyond your orders and the specific confines of your ability. Is that clear, Wes, do we have that clear?

There was a pause, one of those microeternities that conspire to halt a sentence, put a new kink in the universe.

Yes, I finally said to her, we have that clear. But I thought, angrily, you, Chatt, you get to comprehend the big picture, how it works, while the rest of us get confusing fragments, the shatter which we can arrange this way and that.

For an unguarded moment, that moment like a gaze with no defense, I sensed her—almost like it had been, that other time, despite Jessica, when Chatt demanded. In that unguarded moment most-able Chatt let me know how much she could demand.

But if she knew what I thought—if she subtly entered and knew my thoughts and anger exactly as I know them—she chose to ignore as only Chatterley can ignore, for an instant later she was a total stream of facts and figures, a power style as statistical as it comes. She pointed out the drop in the polls Coleman Mosley took after he lost the election and all the stories started coming out about his finagling with his organization Wake Up Planet Earth! Chatt argued that when the so-called democratic process didn't do what Mosley wanted, which was put him in the White House, Mosley would turn against it.

I thought this comment by Chatt was total gall on her part. She knows the democratic process is a sham. If anyone knows that U.S. elections are a sham, Chatterley does. Chatt knows where the real power is in America. Not the people, not the Congress, and no, not The Company, at least not the CIA that exists in government buildings. The workaday CIA is nothing but a collection of college professors and bureaucrats. But The Shop is another beast. The Shop has the power. The Shop is the real CIA that stays hidden beneath the smears and smudges and native greens and red flowers of the budget, of the agency, of the government. The Shop has to have its own hand on the reins. Right now Chatt is that hand.

* * *

The man with the Navajo nose wore a name tag that read: "Hey-Zeus Rodriguez—525." Tall, square-shouldered, long hard cheeks dropping into a jutting Indian jaw, Hey-Zeus stood by the front door of his silver Jaguar four-door sedan, watching me. At first glance he was as stiflingly grim and perfectly out of place as the too-late pallbearer stumbling into church and discovering an early baptism. On second glance—and there was a second glance, an odd, almost crystalline moment—on second glance he fit into The Area like the proverbial missing, indigenous piece. He had pulled his long black hair back into a slick ponytail, a pair of wraparound sunglasses tucked into the straight black shock. He wore black jeans and a turquoise blue long-sleeved shirt with white pearl buttons. A long necklace of silver and turquoise hung around his neck. In a sheath next to his right hip rode a bowie knife. The knife handle was made of yellow bone. "Th' back," Hey-Zeus said with a jerk of his head. I got in. He got in and peered into the rearview mirror with a pair of black pearl eyes.

"Hey-Zeus, huh," I said.

"Yeah. Almost as good as Hey-Venus," he replied. He gave a grunt, then leaned forward and turned the ignition.

Security Detachment Two-Zero was located in the basement of one of The Area's taller green-glass-and-gold-metal skyscrapers. Rodriguez, after sticking a card key into the front door and passing the guard desk in the foyer, walked me down the one flight into the headquarters office. "Adios, newbie," Hey-Zeus Rodriguez muttered.

As Rodriguez left I asked the clerk in the Security Detachment office if Rodriguez was indeed Native American.

"Probably. We got a lot of 'em. We got a lot of everything. You just hired? Who hired you? We ain't had any recent openings, have we? Lemme see your paper." I handed him a piece of paper that had a number on it. The fat man in the gray uniform, who had the make of a former state trooper gone to seed, squinted at the number. He turned to the computer terminal and tapped in a number, going through a menu and a couple of screens. Then he gave a little whistle. "Hokay. You another one of these guys with Euro Division that don't have a name." He glanced at me. "And no, I ain't asking questions."

He tapped the computer and got another menu. "Okay. They gave you digs on base. Nice. Real nice place you got. And seems you got some personal electronic mail waitin' on you. There's a terminal in your room so you can check your E-mail. And before I forget, here's your beeper." He handed me a black, palm-sized telecommunications beeper. "Long beeps, that's a phone call. Bunch of short beeps means you have electronic mail. Two longs and two shorts means report to your Security Detachment headquarters. In that case that's here. Lemme tell you how to get to your room."

They had assigned me an efficiency apartment in the sub-basement. I went down by elevator. A quick count said there were a dozen apartments on the floor.

My efficiency was austere, no attempt being made

to camouflage the practical barrenness with violets and Parisian mystique.

The only sound in the room was the soft chuckle of the ice maker in the minirefrigerator. The blank, square screen of the computer monitor on the counter dominated the room. I could sense the cameras. I could feel the pressure of camera lenses, feel them tense and on my skin. I stowed my flight bag and my one piece of luggage in the closet. There was a jumpsuit uniform in the closet, gray, with a tag. The name tag only had a number: 764. A pair of the black off-road track shoes, the footwear of Mosley's uniformed personnel, lay on the closet floor. I made a show of examining the shoes' thick treads.

Time for the real show: tossing the shoes back into the closet I went to the counter, flipped on the computer, and watched The Great Seal of Mosley blossom in fractal polychromes across the monitor screen. "Push the number two on your keyboard to enter and retrieve your video electronic mail," the computer's alto voice said. So it's video, too, I thought. We get to watch him. I entered and retrieved. Another fractal color burst blitzed the screen, the usual explosive blossoms, and out of the color burst, his image: Coleman Mosley's skin-slick head and notorious grin beneath the broad red handlebar mustache appeared on the high-density screen. I knew I was once again a constituency of one. "Greetings, Mr. Hawkins. I want to welcome you to our organization. You have passed a most rigorous series of examinations and are clearly in the top one percent of the nation in your field of expertise. We only hire eagles at Mosley Synoptics.

"You, of course, will be working in our subsidiary, Global Security Division. Many things are wrong in the world today, Mr. Hawkins, many things that need fixin' and fixin' quick. Peacekeeping, peacemaking, and peace creating are missions that the United Nations clearly is inadequate to meet. Countering the vector of chaos, the global terrorist, is one mission the world's intelligence agencies and police forces have done a damn poor job of, don't you agree? They just aren't up to it, squandering assets, always squandering, pissin' money. If the CIA hadta compete in the private sector, they'd have been out of business a long, long time ago.

"Our evolving global village requires effective security, Mr. Hawkins. Mosley Synoptics, Global Security Division, contributors to Wake Up Planet Earth!, the people of the United States, myself, and now you, are part of the corrective process. I want to thank you for joining with us. I want to thank you for being an outstanding individual ready to contribute to solving the problems plaguing our society and the earth. Thank you for demonstrating the qualities it takes to roll up your sleeves and get the planet's economic engine humming again."

Mosley grinned. The grin filled his face but not his eyes. His eyes focused, blue optics able to penetrate the camera lens, the transmission fibers, the glassy surface of the computer screen. "And God bless you," he said. I could have laughed Mosley's message off as a parody of his presidential campaign, as video egocentrism, if I didn't know the sociopathic facts. At least what Chatt had told me were the sociopathic facts.

The screen blipped and the computer said: "If (slight pause), 764, you have any response to (slight pause) Mr. Mosley's message, please make it now. You may reply verbally or you may type a response. Press the number one for verbal reply, or begin typing."

I knew I had better reply. I pressed the number one.

I said what Chatt had suggested I say: "I plan on doing a professional job, Mr. Mosley."

My first couple of days in The Area were taken up with "in-processing." I took another piss test. I was lectured about drug use four or five times. I said I (Hawkins) had smoked hashish in Chad. The nurse said it was good I could confess.

They took my fingerprints again, as well as a hair sample and a slice of skin for a DNA print. There was another blood test. There would always be blood tests, one of the lab techs confided.

TV screens pop out everywhere in The Area, in hallways, in corridors, in the rest rooms, in the cafeterias and personnel lounges, on the loading docks. Many of the video monitors are tuned to Cable News Network. Some screens continually rerun old *Larry King Live* programs, with King of course interviewing Coleman O. Mosley. Other screens flash glossies of America, pix of gleaming cities and suburbs, farmscapes, forests, idyllic national parks. Then comes the clash: a series of pictures of urban blight and environmental wreckage. Ten thousand white fish bellies bloated on a river in Oregon. The dead fish dissolve to black. Suddenly a blitz of charts erupt on screen, statistics proving to the decimal that America is a step from hell. Mosley appears. From a million screens he vows to get underneath America's hood and replace the engine. Other video sequences appearing on screens around The Area show huge, waving American flags. These are followed by interviews with sports stars and business heavyweights. Then Coleman O. Mosley pops up once more, this time selling success and opportunity. The video screens hawk WAKE UP PLANET EARTH! There are a few bulletin boards, with WAKE UP PLANET EARTH! posters and tacky leaflets promoting recycling and Green Days. There are also a few recruitment posters for the U.S. military.

The "green sequences" in The Area, sometimes referred to as habitats, have a few surprises. While in-processing I investigated one of the green tracts. This particular habitat was located in what was at least a two-hectare-size plot behind the skyscraper next to the building containing Security Detachment Two-Zero's headquarters. I heard a snort and a rush through the brown grass and mesquite thicket. A warthog burst from the underbrush. The ugly tusker shook its head at me. Then, with another burst of speed, he ran straight toward me. He slammed smack into the fine-mesh electrical fence and was flung backward, the electrical shock shaking his body as he tumbled. The warthog got up, shook himself, then plunged forward once again. I saw the warthog do this several times during the two days I in-processed. The wild beast didn't get it. It didn't learn. It couldn't see the fine mesh. To the wild animal's credit, the electric pain failed to quell its instinct to attack.

*   *   *

Security Detachment Two-Zero's headquarters was a nest of video monitors watching the western sector of The Area. It was also a rest home for old men in gray uniforms. None of the men in the Security Detachment appeared to carry firearms. I saw only advanced Taser electric weapons and chemical Mace spray cans and projectors. I did see a guard with an Uzi submachine gun standing in one of the parking lots. In those first two days I never got close to the perimeter of The Area.

I had not thought the security would be so tight. What if I needed special equipment or extraction? If I had to there was always Prism in order to reach Chatt, despite what she had said. If I turned to Prism she would have to respond. I wondered if I was going to spend the next few months in Security Detachment Two-Zero. Mosley had not hired me to police the airport with fat former Georgia state troopers, retired MP master sergeants, and aging ex–Texas Rangers. Still, I did not like the prospect of such an extended operation. Chatt had looked at three or four months. In brief flashes I would miss my daughter, but they were brief. All right, this operation would take time to develop. Peacekeeping, peacemaking, and peace creating. Countering the vector of chaos. No, I had not been hired to police The Area. Unless the area became intercontinental in scope.

On the morning of Day Three there was a knock on my apartment door.

It was Raymond Garcia.

"Can I come in? I see you've finished in-processing."

"Let's hope so."

He sat down in a chair. Arching his dark eyebrows, he said: "Tell me. Straight and no bullshit. Have you formed any impressions about this place?"

"About the airport? It's all very clean. And the security's good. Lots of backup."

"Better than Bolivia."

"There's no comparison. Except we ate as good as you guys and the pay was unbelievable."

"I'll bet. Don't worry about the pay here. You'll be taken care of, Hawk."

So I was Hawk now. With a nickname Garcia had brought me into the gang. "Now that you've in-processed you can get out a little, if you wanta," Garcia continued.

"You mean the new recruits aren't confined to the barracks?"

Garcia chuckled. " 'Guess it looks that way, doesn't it? It's really best for us types to stick around The Area. There's everything here, anyway, everything you need. Take a monorail shuttle over to the mall and the restaurants. There's even an amusement park, y'know, the stuff people need to relax, shooting galleries and killer whales jumping through burning hoops. The monorail line connects to the park over off of I-10. You wanta rub shoulders with the people, you can rub there. No need to go anyplace and fight traffic. Bet you hate fuckin' auto traffic as bad as me, huh, Hawk. Now if you want to kick it back and relax someplace neat and very out of state, catch an air freighter and get there. Heck, when Mosley sets the space station up we'll have space shuttle capability at this base. You'd have to go to Cape Kennedy for the launch but maybe five or six years from now we'll scoot around that. Mosley's got a design for a shuttle launch vehicle that lifts off from the back of a 747 air freighter. Launch has even got recon-strike capability . . . say, you scuba dive, don't you?" He gave me a knowing squint. "Hey, you look like a diver."

I said I had dived once or twice.

"You like to fish? Bet you like to fish." He crooked a finger on the imaginary trigger of an imaginary speargun. "You don't have anything comin' up for a couple of days. The Employer is in Washington and he wants to meet you when he gets back. That'll be a key, buddy. But we can fly down to this island in the Caribbean Mosley owns. Got a big airfield and trade zone area just like this one, except it connects to a beach. Absolutely pure clear water. There's this one bay there where it looks like the boats in it are floating on air."

"No kidding. On the spur of a moment we go to the Caribbean and go spearfishing?"

"Hawk, my naive man. Security work has its perks. The Employer spreads the perks, buddy. It'll take us two and a half hours at Mach 1. We can get hold of the F-5. Do you know about that? Mosley's got a two-seat F-5F. I can fly and you take the back-seat."

"I get a vacation that soon, huh." I wasn't surprised that an ex–Special Forces colonel could fly a fighter. Lots of them were cross-trained. I have qualified in several advanced jet aircraft. Chatterley requires it.

"You need to get an idea of what lies where in Mosley Synoptics. It's real diverse. We'll go down to the island for a day or so. Mosley treats his qualified bodyguards like princes, man. You'll see."

"You're a bodyguard?" I asked. Of course I knew Garcia was. Chatt had that in the files.

Garcia cracked a smile. "Anyone who takes over a foreign security operational slot has to pass Mosley himself. He says if he trusts us to protect him and die for him and keep his body parts together he can trust us to run something out of his eyesight. Then he jokes that nothin' is out of his earshot and eyesight." Garcia chuckled at his own bad wisecrack. "The Employer gets media mileage out of his man of the people act, doesn't he? Anyway, Mosley told me he wants me to get to know you better. Gotta learn to take his hints as what they are."

Chatt had said Mosley's hints were orders. "All right," I said.

Garcia nodded. "If you're wondering why I'd tell you Mosley wanted me to get to know you better, well, Mosley's a genius, see. A genius. America needs a genius, especially with that screw-up Duncan in the White House. Hell, the world needs a genius. But"— as he spoke Garcia lowered his voice to a whisper and faced me, his back to the mirror by the bed, cluing me that a camera lurked behind the glass—"you'll find our Employer's got his downside. He always wants everything checked up on by everything else. You got to play to that trait in him if you work for him and wanta stay sane."

"All right," I said.

Garcia laughed.

* * *

I wanted to take a look at this island, The Island, sooner rather than later. Chatt had satellite photos of it. Worst-case scenario was an ICBM launch point. Most probable case: another "Area" filled with *Larry King Live* reruns, sound bites from *Nightline,* and video monitors.

The F-5 fighter-bomber was stowed at the remote northern end of The Area, where the airport abuts a "green" wildlife area. The wildlife preserve had once been a suburb but Mosley had bought it out, had torn down the houses and schools and convenience stores, and had put in natural plants and species. Vice President Alan Masterson had given Mosley another nifty award for the wildlife restoration.

The Island lay south and east of Cuba. The flight went quickly. At one point Garcia asked me if I wanted to fly the fighter and I said no. I didn't want him to know I could handle a jet. But he insisted so I took the controls and fumbled around, jinking the aircraft. Garcia laughed, then once more took over.

As we approached The Island, Garcia said: "CIA used to have a station here. With Castro down the suck tube of history Mosley bought it."

"He did."

"Yeah. CIA's supposed to need money nowadays. Anyway I think everything's going private. Charity, intelligence, even war."

"Ten billion only buys so much war."

"Ten billion? Oh, Mosley's hoard. He's worth ten billion, I guess. But the organization? Figure a hundred billion at least. Cooperate with a few others and

you triple that, y'know, a few oil Arabs here, a few
rich Hindus there, a Kraut, a Pope and a connected
Jew and an African dictator once in a while. The
organization can buy a lot of war and just enough
peace. Lookit all the chaos. Makes for great live TV,
but every so often stability is good for business."

The Island appeared, the white concrete apron of
the airfield, the emerald jungle set in a ring of white
sand and reef. We banked above the marina, above a
dozen yachts and fishing boats. Garcia brought the
fighter-bomber down, eased up on the controls, and
the landing was gentle, the roll just perfect.

We'd been out on Garcia's favorite fishing boat for
about four hours, a big offshore cruiser with inboards,
bunks for six, and a bar for sixty. Since we had
chugged away from the Synoptics dock Garcia had
drained at least a dozen half-liter Czech eleven degree
beers, one beer after another, a man uncompressing.
"Employer doesn't like drinking, but a man's gotta
blow off now and then, huh?" Garcia had said when
he started. Now, as he tugged awkwardly, drunkenly
on his fishing tackle, a glaze had begun to set in.

"Wanta beer?" he asked for the tenth time. He
scowled at the mess he'd made of the tackle.

"I'll pass."

Garcia quit fiddling with the tackle, took another
long suck at his beer, tossed the empty, and
grabbed a new, icy bottle. He took a slower sip. I
started to . . . I momentarily thought I might
explore the moment, cut through the crap and get
able, inside, but I . . . I didn't. For a moment I

focused . . . but I didn't. I picked the empty up from the deck and put it in the recycle bin. Garcia dropped the rod and reel he was playing with and moved aft. He took over the rod I'd been using.

"So you don't drink, Hawk?" he asked.

"Not much."

"Just communion, huh, I mean you being Catholic. That's where you get your liquor."

"I haven't been to the rail in a while."

"How come? Too exposed up there in front of everybody. Cautious son of a bitch, aren't you. Sure you are, one cautious son of a bitch." Garcia took another long sip from a beer bottle that he'd stashed next to the reel stay. "Yeah, you are cautious." He squinted at me. "Actually, the Employer'll like that. Y'know, I think he was suspicious of you at first, real suspicious. Foreign Legion reputation, like, you were a crook trying to hide a past. But none of that suspicion checked. Y'know why? C'mon, guess. Y'know why? Employer has lines into the CIA, deep lines. N'yup, CIA had some genuine sh-tuff on you, too." Garcia whistled, the whistle shushing between drunken lips. "Man, baby-sitting for a big-ass Nazi war criminal. Gotta be sh-ooper cautious, huh."

The fishing line jerked and Garcia started working the reel. The boat rocked. "Aw, shit. Grab it," Garcia said, his face color a vague mint green. I grabbed the reel and started winding as the ex–Green Beret went to the side and puked.

I reeled in a big grouper of perhaps twenty-five pounds.

"Why don't you lie down, Raymond?"

"Hell, Hawk, lie down—" Bullet Garcia paused

and licked his lips. He steadied himself, or at least tried to steady himself, before he gave in to gravity and plopped down on the deck seat. "Damn. Lesh go back in. You sheem sorta friggin' bored, anyway. You always sheem sorta bored."

"I do?"

"Yeah. Like you kinda seen it all before. Like you're just hangin' around. Is smelling cordite what it takes to get you off, Hawk? Stinging aphro-dishic smell of spent cartridges? I been wonderin' what it takes to get you off." He burped and wiped his mouth on his wrist. "Yeah, I seen guys like you, always lookin' bored. But yer the most looshest goose of all of 'em." He burped again and squinted. "Tell me sumpin'. I gotta know. Didn't you get bored on that Nazi ice mountain in the Andes? Didn't ya? How'd you deal with it up there in the Andes? Howja stay on your toes for those bad Jewboys? Pros, man, Mossad's pro. So if you put it to them you gotta be better than the best."

I started to reply, to tell him what Chatt had told me to say, but before I could give him the perfect response his beeper starting blasting.

"E-mail," Garcia groaned.

"They can ring you out here?" I asked. We were at least six kilometers from the marina.

"There's a relay onna boat." He jabbed a finger at the satellite dish. "There's commo relays everywhere, every friggin' where. Mosley Synoptics is totally wired. The planet's wired, man, you must know that. Can't hide from electrons and satellites so no more fat boy *Reichsführers* ever gonna disappear on Incan glaciers." Garcia cocked a drunken eye. "Indians,

Hawk. You had a deal with the mountain Incas, that's how the Nazi protection contract clicked for so long, right? C'mon and nod. I swore to Mosley you hadda candy deal with the indigenous. I told him that's how you pulled it off." As he wiped his mouth on his wrist he wobbled. "Damn, I'm crocked. You drive this hulk? Then grab the friggin' wheel. I'm gonna answer th' boss."

I went up to the deck, started the engines and punched the anchor button. As the chain stay spun I flipped on the video monitor, selecting the camera in the cabin. There was Garcia, groggy, elbows over the computer keyboard. The camera zoomed to close-up and Garcia looked less drunk, more than angry, the glassy anger alcohol douses and stokes. He turned from the computer and came up to the pilot deck.

"What is it?" I asked. "Your frown starts at your mustache and ends at your ankles."

"Employer said he'll arrive tomorrow to see if all the square pegs are pounded in their proper assholes." The boat shuddered and the engines began their soft thrum. The shudder hit a bad intestinal harmonic: Garcia dropped onto a deck chair, clutching his belly.

As we approached the marina a three-masted yacht appeared to the south. "A-rabs a-hoy," Garcia yawned. "Oh, I need a nap bad, Hawk. What a' afternoon. You nailed a grouper. Guess you get the credit for that kill."

I waited a moment before I replied: "You hooked it, Ray."

"I hooked somethin', man," he groaned.

*   *   *

The cottage they provided me on Mosley's island had a patio facing the beach and the bay. A soft, early evening breeze blowing in from the sea struck a random Oriental melody in the wind chimes which hung just outside the open glass door. Putting down my tumbler of tonic and ice, I walked out onto the red-brick patio. The sun had settled behind the hull of the Arab three-master anchored at the mouth of the bay. Dark red clouds fixed the black silhouette of the sailing ship.

Collecting my skin-diving mask, snorkel, weight belt, buoyancy compensator, and fins, I walked off the patio and down the beach. A thick forest of palms and razor palmettos ran from the chain-link fence encircling The Island's airport all the way to the land edge of the white sand beach. The only breaks in the forest, at least the only breaks I had noticed, were the half dozen other beach cottages, spotted around the bay or on promontories, and the swampy wetlands where the palms disappeared in dwarf cypress and brine. In the wetlands among the reeds heron and tern stalked fish.

I hiked the beach for a kilometer, to a point where it narrowed radically, the thick palm forest an abrupt green wall at my back. I clopped into the warm, shallow water behind the sand break, and I slipped on my weight belt, buoyancy compensator, and fins. I spit onto the faceplate of my diving mask, rubbed the saliva around the glass, then washed it out. When I had a good mask fit around my face I bit down on the snorkel mouthpiece and started swimming toward deep water.

Despite the fading sunlight I could see the sandy bottom with utter clarity. Waves and pools of finger fish schooled in strange dynamic molecules of fins and scales that shifted with the currents, with the sensation of predatory motion in the stands of turtle grass. Small, saucer-eyed stingrays floated through the sand channels like rubber kites with spiked tails. I swam for twenty minutes, further out into the horseshoe bay, diving to the bottom to inspect a conch shell, enjoying the dreamy clarity of the water. I came up for air, blew the salt water from my snorkel, and dived again toward a mound of sand. Lying like a half-hidden star in the sand was a small octopus. As I dove he shot past me with a sudden jet of water and blast of violent ink.

I glanced upward. There was shadow on the surface above me.

I spun—*I had had no notion, no sensation.*

She was floating there, lazily, one hand on a yellow buoyancy compensator, her eyes gazing down into the water, the same remarkable eyes that had startled themselves inside the reflective confines of the Lucky Strikes mirror in Restaurant L'Haut-il. My eyes ran up her long dark legs, over the scarlet monokini, over her naked breasts, to the thin clotted rope of crafted scarification circling her elegant neck.

Does the smell of cordite get you off? Garcia had asked. I been wonderin' what it takes to get you off, he'd burped. Caution keeps me alive, Colonel Garcia, I would have replied, a brutal, disciplined caution.

I watched her watch me. I started to focus, to use my ableness to discover something about this woman, perhaps the glass in the face mask just enough of a prism crystal, but the burn in my lungs overcame my caution and sapped my mental focus. Yes, that's right, that's how it was, blame it on the burn in my lungs.

I kicked to the surface and flipped off my mask. "Hello," I said.

She recognized me. Tossing her long shock of hair back like a mane, she said: "Good evening." The toss didn't last long. The wet hair, like a shawl, collected about her face.

Smiling, I continued a slow kick with my fins, making a semicircular stroke with my arms. During advanced underwater reconnaissance and demolition training I had had to repeat this stroke for twenty-four hours in open ocean, without fins.

"You look relaxed," she observed. "Better than you did in that for-shit dive in Paris." She shifted her weight on the yellow blister of a buoyancy compensator. "Stupid ritual, wasn't it? I almost barfed in the bathroom."

"I'm still trying to find the Frog's Leap."

Nudging a strand of hair away from her face, she rested her chin on the buoyancy compensator. "That's easy," she said with a cocky chill. "When they say frog, you jump." She blinked and tweaked a clinging droplet off the end of her nose. "You the kind of fella who jumps? You got good legs."

I had no insight, no script, and with no inkling apparent I told the truth: "I don't know how to respond to that remark. Flashy retorts aren't one of my strengths."

She startled. Her chin rose, her eyes widened, her breasts left the water then settled once more, touched by the sea. I started to try and focus again, to reach for Chatterley, but I stopped. Yes, my lungs burned.

Peering carefully, the floating woman asked: "Did Mosley hire you?" Then she added before I could answer: "I guess that's an idiot question, isn't it. You wouldn't be here if he hadn't. No one is here unless they're hired."

"I got the job I was after. What about you?"

"Here? Here I'm playing tourist." She flicked a finger toward the three-masted yacht. "Playing tourist for special tourists."

"You swam in from that?"

"No. I'm in a room on the beach. Like you, I suppose. But I'm here because of the ship." She scowled. With a strong kick she started swimming toward the beach. I followed. We reached the sand about the same time. She left the water first, tossing the buoyancy compensator on the sand and leaving it there. With calculated arrogance she walked down the beach, past my bungalow.

As I entered my cottage the beeper started its awful digital Morse. E-mail from Garcia: old Bullet said he was still drunk to his gills and the Gurkha cook at the marina was smoking the grouper. So take it easy, Hawk, my bud.

I tried to take it easy, to shake the oxygen burn in my lungs. I showered, fixed myself a tonic and lime, and went out onto the patio. The sea breeze was accelerating. Thinking about her (I could not quit thinking about her) I walked out onto the beach again, this time into darkness. But one can never assume darkness, not with the available technology, I told myself. Ambient light amplification scopes and goggles magnify and amplify the faintest starlight. On the scope screens and goggle lenses the night world is washed in emerald light.

Try as I might I could not deceive my mind with technology. I thought about her, her breasts against the yellow float, and I made assumptions.

I walked back to the edge of the palm grove and sat down, sipping my drink, the warm sand a tingling velvet.

Sensation—oh yes, sensation, I was open for it, and this time I saw her coming. I watched her approach and heard the pearl crunch of feet on broken shells, a sound with no apparent deception.

She had followed me. "I know your name is Hawkins," she said in a loud whisper.

I was no longer alone with my thoughts and assumptions. Caution, yes, I considered caution, I gave caution ruthless consideration.

But she had dressed and dressed well, her sarong fluttering in the breeze, the dress free where it shouldn't be. I watched, my mind opening, closing around assumptions.

Cautious as a cat she knelt down beside me, her knees sliding from the split in the dress, the scars at her throat like a tight, pebbled necklace I wanted to touch.

"You work with Ray Garcia, don't you, Mr. Hawkins? So you're a bodyguard already. In this organization that's moving up fast."

"I'm not on guard detail. Not yet," I replied.

She placed her hands in her lap. I could feel her reflection on my eyes, her reflection like a ghost with weight. Her curious gaze fixed, as if she were straining to see beyond that self-reflection. Then, as if releasing a hidden magnet, she looked away, toward the sea. "You're not tired, are you?" she said, the pain, the fatigue a subtle curl in her voice.

"Tired of what?" I managed.

Her eyes approached once more, a cool burn of a stare approaching as she draped her long legs out across the keen velvet sand. Her sleek skin reflected the first rise of the moon, the silken, aching porcelain moon.

I did not act on insight or use my ableness, as if I could use my ableness in a moment of obliterating impulse, as impulse overcame me, erased me, impulse like the ultimate command. On an operation I never give into weakness, to impulse. But I succumbed, gave it up as if cursed, pressing a kiss on her thigh, a kiss with sting. The kiss was hot, obliterating, and the passion escaped denial.

I did not even try to deny it, to hide my sudden inability, my loss of discipline.

I lay there. I managed.

"My name is Sari," she said. "Sari. That's my real name. Are you really Carey Hawkins?"

"Yes." That was a lie. And though I was managing it was the first lie I had told in years that felt like a lie. I hated it, the lie, its illness. I had loved the impulse and obliteration.

She kissed me. Obliteration—there was no annihilating tongue but there was no caution, either. The obliteration lingered, delicious lingering inability.

As Sari rolled away and dusted the sand from her dress I managed and coped. Easily, with no reluctance, she placed her hands on mine. "I would rather not . . . no, I mean, not here. I'm sick of that." She looked across the beach, toward the bay. I knew (yes, even without my ableness *I knew* in the way those who adore know) she was looking for that ship, the Arab three-master. She withdrew her hand, her eyes large and wide. "There are monitors, Hawkins, always monitors. But out here we don't . . . I mean . . ." She stared at me, the stare warm yet confused. "Where are you from?" she finally asked.

I knew I had to continue to lie because my life is a lie. "A long time ago Northern Ireland. How about yourself."

"A long time ago Mogadishu. Somalia. Have you ever been there?"

"No," I said. It was another lie.

"You have never been to eastern Africa."

I swallowed. "I didn't say that, did I."

"No, you didn't. No, you didn't say that. Like everyone else you don't say. At one time deceit didn't confuse me. That was once upon a time, before they . . . before my uncle mailed me to them in a yellow taxicab. Now that was a bitch of a day in old New York." She stood and dusted herself off. "Good-bye, Mister Hawkins."

I managed and coped and forced myself—focused myself—to watch her leave. Her walk was elegant, a walk with a pulse to it, a lithe pulse. And when she had disappeared, like all of my best illusions, I threw a shell into the sea, the shock waves appearing from the darkness and lapping at the sand. Then I lay back in the warm sand, lay beside the mark of her body on the sand, the fossil imprint that proved she was no illusion, and I tried to relax, to figure out the pulse, to focus and absorb that pulse, to determine, within parameters, how it was she had been floating above me and I had been so deliciously unaware, a sweet, nonthreatening, momentary loss of my ability. Perhaps in time, with the magnification of a prism, gently, I might engage her, explore . . .

The sensation: Sari's pulse changed to sensation, and I mean *the* sensation, a genuine inkling, the preparatory indicator I had been missing in the sea. Inklings, awareness, hell, I'm talking about ability. You have it, of course, it is you, the sensation of ableness. Ableness brings The Shop to you, that attracting magnet which marks you, scars you, entices them, and then they show you, encourage it, and you develop it, hone it through training, exercise, denial, good discipline, perfecting it their way, the disciplined way.

The able sensation and its quick evolution into awareness relieved me, energized me. Sari returning? No, this wasn't Sari, Sari wasn't able and this signal—yes indeed, I sensed ability, a weak ability attempting to cloak. And suddenly my power was stronger, no, not unfolding manically, like the hotel room psychic burn, but sharp, more able. I sat up, alert, and instantly had the figure back inside the palm forest.

The next second I went down on my belly and began to crawl across the sand spit. Someone able checking up on Sari? On me?

The figure took a step, cannily distributing body weight and pressure, avoiding the snapping resistance of dry palmetto fronds, the giveaway crunch of sand and shell—okay, the stalker can move with stealth. A second step: this one a mistake, hard enough to peg it as a man's step. I rolled up beside a log and reexplored the able sensation, being careful to cloak my power.

He was crouching. He took two more steps and bent slightly.

I finished exploring the sensation and lost all sense of fear and concern. In fact, I was amused, for his ankle was now six inches in front of my face. If he had looked down he would have seen me.

Why hadn't he seen me? Perhaps he was seeing too much. The man was wearing a pair of binocular night vision goggles. He peered around the corner of the palm tree. With the goggles and the power unit strapped to his head (looking somewhat like an open-cockpit-era aviator's goggles) he could have been the genetic hybrid of a human and a microscope.

Mick Fazzari himself, and that explained the sense of an emitter. Chatt had showed me the charts. Mick's ableness was less than one percent of mine. That was the only time she had ever given me a parameter to gauge my own degree of ableness. She was cool about it. No, my ego didn't swell. I knew, from the impression she left, how puny my capabilities must be if compared to hers—

"Down here, Mick," I whispered.

Mick looked down. There was no smile, no joking. With dead seriousness he said: "Damn, man, you're hard as hell to get to."

"Mick—"

"Listen, that beeper of yours. It has a position broadcaster in it. Range of about three hundred meters. Monitoring system tracks to a computer in back of Hangar Five. You got it on?"

"No. It's on my bed."

"Good. Listen. I've got about nine minutes before I'll be missed. So I'll spiel fast. I got here on a contract air freighter, passing as a flight engineer. Ww—" He started to say my name but he stopped himself. "Shit. Man, there's something not right about this operation."

"What."

"I dunno. I can't peg it."

"You came and Chatt didn't send you?"

"That's right."

That doubly explained his attempt to cloak his ability. "Then what's wrong?" I asked.

His mouth skewed. With the goggles he looked like a bitter, glass-eyed monster. "Something is happening near the top."

That jerked me up. "What do you mean?" I considered finding a crystal. . . .

"I don't know what I mean. Something's altered."

"You're not trying to say there's another fight over control in The Shop?! We've settled that."

"Don't rule it out. Check your mission—it's screwy. I'm clued to enough of her process, I've read the infochips. It's a big grab, maybe too big. I say you oughta ice him fast. Waste him fast and git. Maybe she's, you know, in a bonkers fit, a burn. Dark burns, man. She's had 'em. Why the risk, setting you so close? You've thought it. Mosley's a dude big enough to get a piece of The Shop."

I did not reply.

"Look," Fazzari said. "I'm giving you a hunch. I got nothing, man, except twenty years' experience and a thimble's worth of what you got, but it's hunch

enough to have faked my way onto this island and
crawled through a swamp to find you. I intercepted
part of a burst transmission the other night, on my
frequency. It wasn't my code, but you know if I fiddle I
can crack anything. I think The Shop may have
another agent inside Mosley's organization."

"What did you get from the transmission."

"'Watch for Pop.'" Fazzari scowled again. His
goggle-eyes stared at me blinklessly. "On that day
your operational designator was Poppa Four Alfa."

"That may mean nothing or everything."

"You want out now? I could get you on the air
freighter."

I made another decision. "No. Not yet. I've no
indication anything is blown. Chatt would have our
ass. But tell her we should prepare to extract."

"Part of what bothers me is that it's near impossi-
ble to get to you in The Area," Fazzari said. He
looked at his watch. "I've got to run, man. However
this falls out I've rigged an extract kit for you." He told
me where he had placed it in The Area.

I asked about my daughter. I had to ask about my
daughter, her situation.

"That situation's fine. I've got to split," Fazzari
said. "Got to." He gave the beach and the tree line a
glance. Then he looked back at me, his eyes like sudden mirrors. I thought, for a instant, I saw fear.
"Good luck," he whispered. And right then I started
to try, tried to get inside and probe without a crystal.
Fazzari grabbed my wrist and shook. "Stop it, man,"
he said. "Don't get in there, she doesn't want you in
there. I told you, as far as I know your kid's situation's
cool. You don't need to probe, don't need to probe

me. I know my role. I always tell you what I know. Fazzari follows orders, that's hard-wired." I did not reply. He released my wrist. He snapped off a quick salute as he turned and ran down the sandy path into the palm forest.

Five

I knew when I rolled over in the bed that I had slept late. Slats of sunlight split the curtains around the sliding door leading to my villa's patio.

Sometimes the sensation is like that, like a slat of light which slips through and enters, uncloaked.

Now my eyes were open, wide open. Had I been dreaming? Forget dreams, for there can be no dreams, not when I am operational. I glanced toward the front door, waiting, dimly aware. There was a knock at the door and then a second, groggy thud of knuckle on wood. I climbed out of bed.

It was, of course, Ray Garcia and, except for the shave, he looked like sorry hungover hell. "He's here, Hawk," Garcia said. "I mean, you know, him."

"Mosley?"

"The Employer himself. And he's ready to see you. Real ready." Garcia scratched at his chin as he pointed toward the open door.

* * *

The jeep from the island's hangar complex dropped me off in the remote loading sector.

I nodded to the woman standing beside the ramp. I knew her name was Michelle Malone. She was in Garcia's unit. She wore one of the gray jumpsuit uniforms with black cross-country track shoes. Her stiff cherry red hair was closely cropped and brushed back in an angled flattop so that her round forehead above her round face appeared to recede into a perfectly mowed, erect red lawn. She held a black Heckler and Koch MP5 submachine gun. The sub was the silenced model with a laser aiming device and target illuminator. A Taser and a long-range walkie-talkie hung from her combat belt.

"He's waiting on you, Hawk," she said. The white lump of chewing gum snapped in her teeth as she added: "And he doesn't wait."

I walked up the mobile ramp into the big customized 747 Special Performance air freighter.

Another bodyguard stood inside the jumbo aircraft's entranceway. This bodyguard had escaped my notice. He looked to be Vietnamese. He wore a black T-shirt over a muscled chest. "Mr. Hawkins," the man said. "Your knife. Please."

I took my knife from its sheath on the inside of my left calf.

"This is a quality knife," he said. "But you should have told us about it."

"I wear it out of habit."

"There are good habits and bad habits."

"Of course. I'll do better next time."

*　　*　　*

Coleman O. Mosley shook my hand. He had a gleam in his eye. His grip was firm, calipered. "Hot and muggy down here today, isn't it? Makes my mustache droop. Well, South America's just a couple of good spits away." He ran his hand over his bald head. "Make yourself at home. Sit down, yes. G'wan and sit down. Yes sir. Incredible. Simply incredible. Workin' security for a big-ass Nazi. Frustrated Mossad, did you? Those Israelis. Ah'll tell you. Smart, real smart. Have to be. War keeps them on the edge. They're good and honed because they have to be good or they'll die. That's what war does for you. Keeps you lean and on your toes. 'Course you don't want too much of it. Destroys markets. And we're into building markets. Big markets." Mosley pointed to a chair. I sat down. He did not.

Several cabins (rooms is a more applicable description) filled the hull of the air freighter. I had passed through a meeting room, complete with phones and oval desk, through a small galley, to what was clearly Mosley's office. The air freighter was not all that different from Air Force One, the U.S. president's airborne command center.

This office included a desk (with a picture of Mosley and a young man I knew to be his son, both of them standing next to a television set), several chairs (all bolted down, all padded, all with seat belts), various telephones, computers, and a model train set.

Mosley walked over to the model train yard. He turned a transformer. Two or three engines started to roll, clicking around the convoluted tracks. "Can I getcha something to drink, Hawk? No? That's right, you don't drink. Good habit. Are you having a good time?" Mosley's face wrinkled, his big nose flattened. He chuckled. "Ray Garcia had a little too much good time, didn't he? Hasn't learned he shouldn't pollute his body. Cleanliness is next to godliness." One of the engines whistled, rushed past Mosley, then entered a long tunnel. "You like trains? Never thought about them much, huh. 'Course not. Well, come on over and look. C'mon, Hawk."

I got up and came over. I stood behind the round-house.

"Now this here layout ain't historically accurate. It's not like my layout at my ranch up near Montana. You never been out to the ranch, have you? We'll have to have you. You can meet the grandkids. Yessir, Hawk, family, nothing like children and family, is there?"

Another engine shot past, something black with a smokestack. "Now this yard over here is based on an old New York Central yard outside of New York City. It's modeled on the robber baron era, y'know, Astors and Morgans and Rockefellers, all of them battling over the cornerstones of the industrial age. It was a time of blood and iron, Hawk. Men with nicknames like Diamond Jim and Big Jack. You heard of the Pennsylvania, the New York Central, the Erie and Lackawanna. The railroads battled, destroyed one another, ultimately incorporated out of their destruction. Ended up the Penn Central, then the Consolidated Rail Union." Mosley gave the transformer a twirl. Another engine, followed by a coal car and two empty flat cars, flew out of a tunnel. "I could have a computer do all of this, of course, I mean, ours is an age of brains and sili-con, ain't it. But there's nothin' like keeping your own hand on the throttle. Whyn't you take over for a spell, Hawk? G'wan."

I took the throttle on the transformer.

"Now watch it. Not too much juice."

I turned the power down. An ancient engine with a cow catcher chugged down the straight. It pulled a single Wells Fargo bank car with the sign SAN FRANCISCO GOLD hand-painted on its side.

"Aw. You can give it more than that, can't you?"

I upped the power. The engine moved a bit faster.

Mosley cocked an eyebrow. "You're the always-careful type, huh. Have to be, I guess, if you're showing desert tribesmen how to draw a bead on someone's head. Lemme show you." Mosley took over the transformer. As he stepped near me I got a whiff. It smelled like he was wearing Vitalis on his mustache.

The engines began to fly around the closed infinity of the figure-eight track. I had completely lost the sense that we were in the modified cargo bay of an air freighter.

"Now," Mosley said as he flipped a lever and switched trains onto different tracks, "the Pennsylvania and the Erie and the New York Central all fought for dominance of rail traffic to the Midwest. Dominance, Hawk, as in domination." Mosley goosed the transformer. The engines whined. "But the poor bastards were tied to their own systems, to their trackage. Look what happens, Hawk, when you're tied to trackage, when you can't get flexed and live without rails. Observe the little engine that could, the one with the Wells Fargo gold car tagging its ass. And from the tunnel the big bad Chicago Express."

Mosley must have flipped another switch. Here

came a gray steel engine with about forty power wheels, the engine flying out of the tunnel with a banshee whistle. From the opposite direction the engine with the big cow catcher on its chin and the gold car entered the straightaway section of track.

The trains crashed into one another, the Chicago Express skidding into the side of the roundhouse, the antique engine and the Wells Fargo car flipping off the layout into Mosley's palm.

The engine and the car were really quite small.

"And a microtragedy," Mosley mused. He put the engine back on the tracks. "Railroads sped up time in their era, Hawk. Distance in the world shrank from weeks to days. Now, well, we're moving a little faster, wouldn't you say?" He put the Wells Fargo gold car back on the tracks and gave it a nudge. "Got to stay flexible, Hawk. Running things around on tracks is a lesson in flexibility. Tracks only go over the same terrain. If we're gonna compete in this new age of economics you got to push out, seek new concepts, sell alternatives. Right now we're fighting over the cornerstones of fortunes in the information era, yessir. We got to escape the tracks some of us are on in our minds and we've got to escape the political tracks some folks seem hellbent on taking. Virtual, Hawk. MIT and Harvard don't know it yet. Their brains might fidget right but their organizations are glaciers. The present and future belong to the flexible, Hawk, those that know what's out there"—Mosley tapped his head—"and know how to organize it th' fastest."

Mosley turned the transformer off. "Well. A little relaxation." He grinned and his ears wiggled with planned friendliness. "I wanted to look at you myself, Hawkins. I've checked you out real well. Baby-sittin' a bigwig Nazi and getting away with it. And nothin' getting out to the press. Yessir, I wanted to meet you face-to-face. We can do lots of things electronically. You seen that. Computers add to efficiency. But computers don't replace old palm grease and a firm handshake, do they? Y'know all the old paranoid Big Brother stories folks used to write, about computers dominating the world? Horseshit, ain't it? A computer is just a tool. You follow me? Just a tool for people to use. Take the blind. Computers can see for them. The deaf? To a point computers can hear for them, y'know, detect and construct usual conversation."

(For a moment, a second, I thought of Jessica, her stutter, but being operational, I killed the thought.)

" 'Cause these are technical corrections, Hawk. Mere technical corrections on the biology. That's the way we're approaching that problem at Mosley Synoptics. We see a problem, we try to fix it. But computers aren't running anything. You follow me? Do you?"

He stared at me. I felt awareness. *Yes, I knew as it occurred, an inkling.* "And y'know," Mosley said, "that's the thing that galls me about President Duncan and his palavering. He palavers, don't you think? There's a big difference between flexibility in achieving a goal, Hawk, and dodging. Randy Duncan don't know how to fix anything. Bosnia. Look at how he botched Bosnia. Ireland. You're Irish, right? From Northern Ireland. Peace? Baloney. More time fer those micks to build bombs. And I mean th' micks on both sides, if you don't mind the expression. Terrible situation, the sectarian violence."

I nodded.

"What do you think about that, Hawk."

I went for soldierly inarticulateness: "People should leave each other alone."

"Ever go into Catholic neighborhoods?" he asked.

"I am Catholic," I said. I did not like the exploratory look in Mosley's sharp eye.

"Oh yes. Right. Well then, into Protestant ones."

"Yes . . . I left there when I was twelve," I said.

"Right. For Australia, Texas, and other places. You been around. Well, I understand that. I was born in Arkansas and I had to get the hell out of Arkansas. But Arkansas isn't a bad place to be from. . . . Sometime we must discuss those other places you've been. In detail. I enjoy details." Mosley stretched out another smile. His eyes twinkled. He put his hand on my shoulder. "Okay. I'm comfortable with you. And that's good. So we'll discuss some more things back in San Antonio. Such as those peacekeeping, peacemaking, and peace creating missions that the United Nations clearly is inadequate to tackle. But we're talkin' to the U.N., talkin' right now. With the right palm grease and right facts we may be some private guys doin' worldly work. You and reliable personnel like you will be part of the solution."

He glanced toward the door and slapped me on the shoulder.

I took the hint.

I spent the rest of the day on The Island, agitated but feigning enjoyment of sand and sea. I did not find Sari and there was no second visit from Mick Fazzari. Late that evening I climbed into the F-5 with a sobered Garcia and we flew back to The Area. I admit I considered punching the ejector seat and bailing out of the operation, literally. I had listened to Fazzari. Mosley had asked questions I found transparent and leading. I considered using Prism, pushing the ability, but decided against it. Chatterley's orders—they remain paramount, always. We arrived in The Area and Hey-Zeus Rodriguez took us to our quarters.

The next morning I was officially assigned to the Bodyguard Detachment, though I did not meet any of the other bodyguards. I was told I would keep my own efficiency apartment in the Security Detachment Two-Zero headquarters building. The only other event of note was that afternoon when I joined, at Garcia's order, Mosley's internationalized political and environmental organization, Wake Up Planet Earth! The twenty-five-buck donation would be taken from my first paycheck.

The day after joining Wake Up Planet Earth! I did get a look at some of the other bodyguards as they worked out in the gymnasium. The guards were an impressive lot. Several of the men were ex–Green Berets or Navy SEALs. The three women were ex-FBI. There was an emphasis on discipline and cleanliness (bath a day, shower after every workout). They all took their daily piss tests.

Chatt had clued me: a couple of the bodyguards had worked for the CIA but never inside The Shop. How many times must it be said before the truth escapes the lies? There is CIA and then there is The Shop. There are those who think they know who is what in global intelligence activities. Those who think they know get to pose before congressional committees, to leak to the press, to posture in boardrooms, and then are interrogated at the White House. But ultimately there is The Shop, its secrets, its storehouse of ability. Some presidents don't get to discover The Shop. Take President Grover Renwick, for example. Renwick served as director of the CIA, but he was too squeaky clean and lacked essential perceptive qualifications to be engaged by The Shop. Renwick had no ableness. Can you imagine Renwick approaching a crystal, trying to use Prism? President Nixon? Now Dick Nixon had a glimpse of The Shop, a glimmer, and when he started to get suspicious, to hound about, well, The Shop protected its prerogatives. Carter? Jimmy Carter flinched at rabbits. Reagan? Reagan didn't know a damn thing, but Bill Casey, his director of CIA, did. Casey had the necessary qualities. Ability? If anyone can communicate from beyond the grave it's William Casey. But Casey communicated too much, that's what Chatt said anyway. Casey joked that he could see the bones of those of us who had been buried so deeply. He let on that he knew, he let on to snoopers and he let on that he knew too much. The next generation of The Shop, my generation, an improving generation with increased gifts and abilities—my generation knew that Bill Casey put the whole damned Shop at risk. Casey knew why he got sick. Casey knew why he was dying when he was dying. He knew what brought the obliterating cancer, what caused the final stroke.

*   *   *

I was eating lunch in the cafeteria reserved for the Bodyguard Detachment and some of the old coots in Two-Zero when Garcia walked in. "You wearing your beeper?"

I said I was. To prove it, I gave it to him.

Garcia scowled and flipped the widgit over a couple of times. "Well, Mosley's in his office and he's been looking for you for an hour. Maybe the battery's bad. I'll get you a new one. You better hustle over to his office."

I finished my glass of iced mint tea.

The Vietnamese bodyguard smiled when I handed him my knife.

As I entered the gold-carpeted office Mosley punched a button. Whatever he had been viewing on the wall-sized television screen faded instantly to black emptiness.

"Hawkins. Take the chair."

I thought Mosley sounded a bit nervous, but it may have been his bantam energy. There was the glint of sweat on his bald head. Funny, odd—I felt a sense of anticipation, a preparation.

Mosley bit his lip, then said: "You're Irish, right? Hell, you had the nickname Irish in the Legion. We checked on that. Well, you know, the Irish helped make this country great, didn't they, Hawk. They were immigrants who came to work. . . . immigration is a tough problem, isn't it? Legals, illegals, some come here just to get on the dole, but others pick up the slack in the economy. Tough problem. Lots of slack around. But we're working on solving it. The people are telling me it's a problem and I'm listening."

A soft buzz, not unlike the buzzer on the telecommunicator code phone in my own office, went off.

Mosley glanced at his watch. "Hold it." He went and sat down behind his desk, punched a button on the computer keyboard built into his mahogany desktop, and the black wall brightened.

"Ah, the grandkids. My son's kids. You ever see my son, Hawk?" Mosley nodded at a framed picture standing on his desk. "No? Never met him, huh? Maybe you'll meet him someday. You should get to know the family. We're family here."

Smiling child images filled the video wall's dense pixels.

"Happy birthday, Grandpa," a half dozen child voices shouted. On the screen the children expanded, larger than life-sized. Mosley spoke with the kids for a moment, a patter, then said he had to get to work. "Make sure you say howdy to your daddy, hear?" Mosley grinned. The children said good-bye, one by one. The screen went dark.

"Family structure is important, Hawk. Families. I tell you, I love my son and I rely on him. . . . What kind of family did you have?"

"Not much."

"But a sister, right. Killed by an IRA bomb."

"Yes, Mr. Mosley."

"Must have scarred you."

"I'm the kind of man that ends up in the Foreign Legion, Mr. Mosley."

"Right. Of course. No denigration meant. I'm a curious fellow. . . . Anyway, here's where I'm headed this morning." He punched another button on his keyboard. Part of the wall opposite the big-screen television parted. Another screen emerged. "This is for classified transmission, Hawk. Fancy, ain't it. High pixel density on very thin video. Exciting technology. Images on this screen flow as warm as movie film. Y'can almost worship stuff this great. Watch." A picture of President Duncan flashed onto the screen. Duncan stood behind a podium, hands raised, mouth moving. But there was no sound. "Now, this is what the country has come to, ain't it. You are familiar with America, aren't you? You came to Texas early, you say, but then got around elsewhere? Duncan. Man, what promise gone a mess. But Renwick—I hated him, Hawk. Renwick . . . Renwick was a dumb bastard."

The president disappeared. Duncan was replaced by a picture of the first lady. She stood there, motionless, like a statue. "Mrs. Duncan. Now there's a piece of work."

He waited. I didn't say anything.

"Dangerous woman in my estimation. Dangerous. Wants to be president herself. I'm not against women. I promote them, yessir, I've demonstrated that. But . . . something about her. Look at those eyes. Like she's gazing past you, through you, beyond you. You ever get that feel?"

I did not reply.

Another picture formed on the screen. "Vice President Masterson. Fine man. Exquisitely fine man. Recognizes *quality* in people. Understands the planet needs to be healthy. You have a healthy planet, you have healthy people and a healthy state of mind.

Good ecology leads to good psychology, Hawk, it sure do. And he's beginning to appreciate the role of technology in that cycle. Ecology, technology, psychology. Master those and biology ain't ever gonna pose a problem." Masterson disappeared, replaced by a picture of President Duncan with his arm around his son. "Utter flabbergastation. Duncan . . . okay, we've had a few skirt chasers running America. But he shows up on posters with that boy of his, using that boy. White House press people show this stuff to deflect the truth. Poor kid. Look at those thick glasses. What an icon of family values."

"I understand the young man has a gifted intellect."

"Takes after his mother there, I guess," Mosley sniffed.

A new picture took the screen. "Former president Renwick, a Republican. That should say it, huh? Now, this man tried to have me shadowed by the CIA." Mosley smirked. "Hell, CIA owes me more than it does him and the fool was once the director. Republicans, those stuffed shirts only think about money and capital gains. 'Course now business is the engine of America, I'm not disputing that, but greed isn't. Greed kills surer than speed. My grandmother used to say that money was just another way of spelling greed so having money amounted to possessing greed. Greed's a sin. That means being a Republican's a big sin, you comprendo? Catholics still have sin, don't they? Well, Grandma would tell me about the sin of greed, then she'd give me a quarter and tell me to go spend it on ice cream. I didn't spend it. I saved it. Ended up with a lot of money. That isn't greed. Grandmothers can be wrong,

Hawk." Mosley grinned. "I use my quarters to save the people. You follow me."

"Yes."

"Good. Now stay up. We move fast at Mosley Synoptics." He pushed a new button. "Now what is that?"

"That is a fifty-caliber sniper rifle," I said.

"Model?"

"It looks like an L82, sir. Made by Barrett Firearms of Tennessee."

"Yes indeed. Barrett. A fine weapon. What do you know about that rifle?"

"It has an eleven-round magazine. Other than that, not very much."

"But for being on a Nazi mountain you are pretty well informed about some of the new gadgets."

"We got all of the defense magazines."

"I'm sure you did. We checked. We're still looking for Mr. Portales, by the way."

"When you find him, say hello, would you?"

"For sure, for sure. Let me tell you something about the L82, for future reference. The L82, an update of the famous L2, holds the world's record for the longest confirmed single-shot sniper kill. During a certain fiasco in Somalia this little doozy punched out a kill at nineteen hundred meters. A Green Beret behind a dune dropped a clansman. The hit's on videotape by the way, so we've got instant replay. A clean single shot, technology and finesse, and by damn you can follow the ballistic path from flash to strike. . . . Could you make a shot like that?"

"Depends on the conditions, Mr. Mosley. In the desert you can get unobscured lines of sight."

"Clear LOS, huh, to imbibe of the jargon. Okay, I'll buy that. Now what do we have here . . ."

Another bit of death technology appeared on the screen, luminous and shining as if materializing from evil vapor. But don't let the technoglitz fake you: the death technologies only exist to kill and terrify, to either gain or retain power. They have no magic.

"That is a Lincar Laser Six optical designator, ballistic computer, and targeting system," I replied. "You can mount it on a sniper rifle and dramatically improve your chances of a first-round hit."

"Dramatically, huh . . . can you use it?"

"Yes."

"You put the laser light on the target, get a reflection off the target that accounts for ammunition drift and gravity, and then you pull the trigger. Real useful in shooting, huh, Hawk?"

"Shooting is more than technology, Mr. Mosley."

A short whistle broke from his pursed lips. "Ooooweeee. But ain't it, though? Got to have those other legs of the triad. Ecology and psychology. Then you add an opportunity and the will." Mosley stared at me. A smile appeared beneath his handlebar mustache. "You following me? Or are you wondering where this is going?"

"I'm trying to follow you, sir."

"Good. I want you to follow me, Hawk, I want that very much. Well, that'll do it for now. I've got a birthday party waitin'."

"Yes, Mr. Mosley."

* * *

Mosley was suspicious, too suspicious and too cocky. Still looking for Portales, huh, still grinding away on Chatt's cover story. Fazzari suspected something had changed. Common sense informed me I had already been compromised, so I decided to ditch the operation and get out. I went back to my room and found a new beeper sitting on the desk. As I stared at it, wondering if it contained a special transmitter or a small bomb, I thought through a dozen possibilities, including escape on one of the trucks or theft of an air freighter or fighter-bomber. Fazzari said he had pre-positioned an extraction kit, which would help if I had to hijack transportation. I closed my eyes, waiting for a sensation, my fist closing on an imagined crystal. *And there had been the faintest essence of sensation, then more, those dark mirrors . . .* curious, I thought, perhaps Fazzari? I tried again—blocked, nothing.

I panicked, then coped with my panic. With each inkling screaming that the operation had gone to rot, I desperately wanted a Prism contact with Chatt, at least the possibility of psychic reinforcement if not enlightenment, but she, the ultra-able commander, had denied that conduit. Could a contact compromise The Shop? I am supposed to die before compromising The Shop. I am a soldier. I understand that. I must cope . . .

The door buzzer: I felt a quick sense of anticipation, of ability, but it faded, no, it died. The buzzer again: I opened the door, expecting Garcia.

The Navajo, Hey-Zeus Rodriguez, stood in the doorway, backed by another dozen members of the Bodyguard Detachment, all dressed in black jumpsuits, all lugging MP-5 submachine guns.

"You wearing that fine knife?" one of the body-guards asked.

"Yes."

"Then you must take it off," Hey-Zeus Rodriguez said. His right hand rose and rested on the butt-end of his bowie knife. "For you, at the order of our Employer, are under temporary arrest."

Six

Temporary arrest? The arrest smacked of permanency. Had *they* been reading my mind? Only Chatt knows my mind. There had been no indications or a probe, just that vague inkling . . .

The arrest had the smack of permanency but not the sustaining pain. There was . . . there was a continuing sensation, a perplexing sort. I knew I had to ask why I had been arrested. I asked why because I knew if I didn't make some fuss I would be completely suspect. There had to be, on my part, the perception of resistance.

They were not gauche enough to put me in handcuffs. I followed one of the bodyguards. We left the building and headed for Hey-Zeus Rodriguez's silver Jaguar. Did the Navajo have one of these cars at all of Mosley's bases? I sensed nothing. I got zero. Ability can be like that. That's why you have to be ready to operate without it

As we drove I asked Rodriguez if I were being taken to a prison in The Area, or would be flown to The Island, perhaps? We were heading for the flight line.

"Naw, naw," Hey-Zeus Rodriguez replied as we climbed out of the silver Jag. We stood before a row of two dozen 747 air freighters. "The world's prison enough, isn't it, Hawkins?"

A few moments later Mosley's Cessna Citation X transcontinental business jet rolled out from behind the air freighter flight line. The members of the Bodyguard Detachment, Rodriguez, and I climbed on board the jet.

I sat next to Michelle Malone and noticed she had a canine tooth tattooed on her right earlobe, the lobe poking from beneath a lick of her cherry hair. She didn't look at me and she didn't say anything. She stared straight ahead. I cleared my mind. My mind would not clear. The jet engines whined and the jet took off.

About a half hour after we were airborne Hey-Zeus stood, stretched, then came to my seat. He leaned across Michelle. I noticed a large crystal, a pendant teardrop on the turquoise and silver necklace that swung from his thick bull neck. I had not noticed the crystal before—how in Hell's name had I missed it? I made certain I did not stare at the perfect crystal.

"We won't have any trouble out of you on this flight?" Hey-Zeus asked in a tone that was as much order as it was question.

"No," I replied.

He turned away.

I looked at the crystal as it swung away from his chest.

Utter coincidence, of course, no screaming reason to suspect anything, to calculate suspicions otherwise. Native Americans kept those things, those haunting edges. They are charms, these crystals, mere tokens kept for luck. They are quartzite and faceted geologic relics that spark when dangled in the light, that break light into its streaming spectrums.

I waited for a sensation. I kept waiting until the emptiness began to turn to panic.

The crystal was coincidence, I concluded as I pressed against the window and looked out over the ocean of white clouds.

We refueled in Gander, Newfoundland. We took off again, racing across the Atlantic. The next stop was Belfast, Northern Ireland. I felt Mosley's trap closing and I desperately wanted to turn to Prism.

Belfast: We clambered out of the jet. The clouds were gray and low, the drizzle sticking to your face like a slow, cold sweat. The bodyguards left their weapons on board, or at least they left the submachine guns on board beneath the seats.

We went through customs and passport control in the air cargo terminal. The customs officer asked one of the bodyguards why we had no baggage. "Our flight's continuing on. We're just getting off to look around," was the reply. "You think we could spend some money? You know, spread a little foreign exchange?"

A burgundy red Jaguar was waiting for us outside the air cargo terminal. Hey-Zeus took the wheel as the two male bodyguards sandwiched me in the backseat.

"Tell us how to get to the old neighborhood, Hawkins," Michelle Malone said as she climbed in the front.

I begin to visualize. In my preparation to portray Hawkins I had viewed over two hundred slides of places in Northern Ireland. It was quite possible I knew some street corners better than natives. I knew the street maps well. I had not only memorized the contemporary street map but I had burned into memory a street map of thirty years ago. There were slight differences, the subtle disparities a detail freak like Mosley would have analyzed and accounted for.

"Drive on into the center of Belfast and let me get my bearings," I said as we left the airport.

"Why should we?" Michelle Malone snapped.

"Shut up, you idiot," Hey-Zeus Rodriguez said. He glanced into the rearview mirror, his black eyes bright and hard.

The neighborhood was dirty, dingy, begrimed with the squalor of working class sweat and industrial soot.

"Turn here," I said.

The neighborhood was a materialization of what I had visualized. I recognized several tenements from the recon photos and computer simulations.

"Okay. Where's your family's house?" Rodriguez asked.

"It was destroyed in the explosion."

"And you haven't been back since you were twelve?"

"Yes. Age twenty. I went to my sister's grave."

"You did not attend her funeral."

"I was in Australia."

"We're checking on that," Michelle Malone said.

A fresh map conjured in my mind. Maps stay in

my memory, like the patterns of fascinating circuits remain in the minds of gifted electrical engineers. Perfecto—I recognized the entrance to an alley on the left. "Turn right," I said. "The next street."

The street, walled with dirty brown and red row houses, ended in a carnage of blown-out buildings, graffiti, and scattered bricks. Children played among the ruins.

"You're sure this is home," Michelle Malone said nastily.

"Practically," I replied.

"What do you mean?" Rodriguez asked. He held a palm-sized computer in his hand.

"I mean I haven't been here in twenty years or so. Let's get out. . . . I'd like to see it."

We got out of the car.

Of course I had never seen the street before, except in my imagination and in Chatt's files.

"You're sure?" Rodriguez asked.

"Be damn sure," Michelle Malone said.

A man on a crutch hobbled off of a house stoop, his stiff gallop convincing. As he reached our group he stopped and peered into my face.

The makeup job was excellent, but I recognized his eyes, despite the contact lenses, and the contour of his face. The man with the crutch was Mick Fazzari.

"Carey Hawkins? Is it you? Remember me?"

Fazzari was affecting a clear, bright Irish accent.

"No," I said.

"Seamus McNamara."

"Oh." A smile broke across my face. "Yes. My God. It's been years. How did you recognize me?"

"You look like your father. What are you doing here? Who are these dour people?"

"Some folks I've done some security work for."

"Security work?" Fazzari scowled an excellent scowl.

"Private. I do not work for the British."

"Why, I wasn't thinking that." Fazzari-McNamara leaned on his crutch and peered toward the Jaguar. He gave Rodriguez a careful scan.

"What happened to your leg."

"A product of the troubles," he replied. "Not much like the old neighborhood. It's missing some teeth. Bloody fucking Brits." Fazzari grinned.

"I thought an IRA bomb did this," I said, pointing to the rubble.

"The Provys? Yes. It was. You remember Aquinas Connor? He ended up making a few bombs in his cellar." Fazzari chuckled.

No one else did.

"Well. You've seen us. Would you want to come into my place for a drink or go down the block a bit? No, it isn't so far. You walk and I'll make up."

The pub smelled of ale and men who smelled of ale.

We sat at an oak table at the rear of the pub. The table consisted of me, Rodriguez, and Fazzari. Rodriguez had told Malone and the others to wait outside.

"Do I order two or three pints?" Fazzari asked.

"I'll pass," Rodriguez replied.

"Coffee," I said. "Black."

"Ah, you're your father's son. He was a man never much for ale or pubs," Fazzari said, shaking his head perfectly, his eyes brightening with false memory and faked delight spurred by an invented history.

Fazzari ordered a pint and a cup of coffee. The drinks came and I sipped my coffee as Fazzari went through a convincing spiel about a dozen people from the local neighborhood, where their lives had gone, which ones had already died. I'm sure he gleaned the locals' names from one of Chatt's files, or, if this cover operation were really thrown together quickly, from names on mailboxes.

Rodriguez looked bored. Someone had started the jukebox over in the corner. You would expect an Irish jig but the song was one of those pompous protest songs about new world chaos and CNN. *Cable wired, a world apart, the war is live and the bombs are smart.* Rodriguez turned and glanced at the jukebox.

I was certain Rodriguez had a tape recorder or some kind of microphone on him—he had a sensation about him—so the Navajo surprised me when he excused himself, stood up, and walked over to the jukebox, then walked into the john in the back.

I pulled my beeper out and stuck it under the table, smothering it beneath the sole of my shoe, just in case the beeper had a mike built into it.

"How the hell did you get in position to pull this charade off."

"Chatt. Guess she isn't bonkers, huh."

"Does she have Mosley Synoptics tapped or has she, uh, put her brain into his, maybe?"

Fazzari chuckled. "I'd guess The Shop has his operation tapped. But you'd know more than me about the more pernicious means of gaining real-time intel, wouldn't you?"

I didn't reply. I think I grimaced. What's real-time about the mind, and what's more frigging uncertain? Okay, Fazzari had ability, but a stunted ability. He is very limited, almost unable. I bit my lip and thought: *Bits and pieces of your great information, is that all we deserve, Madame Chatterley?* If I had had a prism I would have burned it into her.

Fazzari blinked. A word started to form on his lips but did not. Then Fazzari continued, as if he had never stopped speaking: "Chatt says Mosley suspects you're a plant."

"No kidding . . . cut to the chase. Do I get out now?"

"She says no dice. Stick with it. Lookit the effort she took to get me here to reinforce your shaky cover." Then Fazzari slipped me an object that looked like a woman's lipstick container.

"I need to talk to Chatt."

"She says no Prism contacts permitted. She says Mosley is about to buy something big, move things around. And The Shop does have someone besides you on the inside."

"But she won't say who it is."

"No."

"Look. Look at me." He looked. "Mick—am I to kill him?"

"Goddamn, man. You know riff raff like me can't

discuss wet details. That's between you and The Shop command."

Between me and The Shop command.

When Rodriguez returned I excused myself and made the trip to the rest room. I went into a stall. The lipstick container held lipstick, all right. It also had a light emitting diode message window in its butt. Three turns and the LED window lit. A dozen alfanumerics appeared in the window, the pattern telling me this message was from Chatt. Was she avoiding Prism? I asked myself. Chatt's most-able powers are stream powers—so utterly rare—where the flow is always there, always available to some degree, fluctuating perhaps but not intermittent. That is why she is who she is, why she is where she is. I looked at the LED. I felt afraid. Obviously she wanted to be certain that this message was received with utter clarity. Okay, contacting me telepathically, should I resist and screw around, must require more of Chatt than she wants to apply. But at the moment, in that john, there was no resistance. *There has been no real resistance, then, now.* I was her soldier. *I am her soldier.* I was not resisting, I wasn't screwing around. I was operational in an operation going rotten. I was afraid, discipline crashing, and fear does things. Perhaps that change, I thought, perhaps she's picked up on the change—*she knows the change*—in that goddamn Paris hotel room. Oh, man, I thought, *gild mirrors like ice around you,* confused, disoriented, time disjointed. Without harsh discipline and training, ability can get chopped up in time. I cloaked. That helped. Fear subsided and I got steady. Then I started to focus. The thing is, when I am alerted, Chatt knows I am extremely receptive, extraordinarily able to respond. I squeezed the LED. Chatt knows I'm a lesser creature, stunted and limited. But my experiments, that god-damn change. Yeah, the experiments, those episodes of rebellion she holds against me. I stopped focusing. Read the message, I thought. So I read it. "The next two weeks are critical. Stay with it. Be prepared to follow Mosley's instructions. Your daughter is fine."

Follow Mosley. Well, Chatt knows. She could read my mind. She could, after all, enter. Could she direct? Did she direct me? Place, enter, direct. She had the spectrum of abilities. And she knew me, didn't she? She knew I could be weak. She addressed my weakness, my cherished weakness.

"Your daughter is fine." Yes, I could almost hear Chatt place those words in my mind.

An acid released by one further twist of the lipstick tube burned out the microbattery and microcircuitry and turned them into silicon goo. The black LED window dissolved to gray. I flushed the lipstick down the toilet.

If I could read her mind like she does mine.

Chatterley. There are reasons someone with her powers now leads The Shop. The *New York Times* and the *Washington Post* have covered much of this in detail, vis-à-vis the ancien régime in Moscow. The Russians, when they were still the Soviets, spent three decades pushing the limits of the mind, going into the most bizarre and macabre and extraordinary skills of our human mental apparatus, attempting to define, understand, then exploit (as a weapon, as a weapon for penetrating secrets, as a weapon for keeping secrets, as a weapon of death and destruction) those tantalizing powers of the brain humankind has known to exist since time immemorial. Which powers? Those powers that create our saints and devils, those paramental capacities that inhabit all of us but are forces and skills appropriating forms and patterns that the dry schematics of Western, Eurocentric science fail to account for, much less comprehend.

The construct of Western science even works to suppress research into these fundamental capacities. Not so those seeking advantage, not so those who know the value of insight, the value of harnessing weapons to your cause. Our former adversaries understood the value of weapons. Sorting through the hoke and quackery of myriad fakes and charlatans, the Soviet program, a KGB program run by the First Chief Directorate's Advanced Language Institute (a cover name for the KGB branch devoted to special intelligence projects), plunged deep into a host of paranormal phenomena.

Telekinesis came under particular Soviet scrutiny, the ability to move objects by acts of mental effort and will. Once identified, could this skill be refined, sharpened, intensified? Marbles moved on a chess board ("pushed" telekinetically by individuals exhibiting paranormal talents) were one thing, a parlor game, an exhibit for carnivals, little more than the magic of gifted gypsies and housewives. A single die flipped from one side to another on a gridded, digitized Plexiglas table in a research center, flipped by paranormals concentrating in a controlled laboratory environment, was cause for excitement. The academic gods of chance, of the damning schematic of mathematics and mathematical explanation, were being squeezed back into their corner. But, the Soviets quietly asked, can we use this in the struggle, can an operative exploiting these capabilities twist the laws of chance in a casino, inside the random number generator software of a U.S. National Security Agency crypto-computer?

Soviet results were significant. There were break-throughs, utterly fantastic breakthroughs. But in general the Sovs did as terrible a job of exploring and then exploiting these extraordinary human capabilities as they did in fighting the rest of the Cold War. Psychic KGB spies, what a laugh, a short feature in the tabloids, more headlines for the dust-bin of history. The Soviet institutes, like all Soviet efforts, had exceptional personnel. They verged on decisive insights. But they never found their Chatterley. They never found a genius like a high-tech witch, able to vibrate a crystal, able to run her ideas through a network of silicon chips, able to amplify them in your mind, able to shape pliant wills, able to know what needed to happen, a genius with the guts to make it so.

"Seamus," I said as I stood beside the door to the bur-gundy Jaguar.

McNamara-Fazzari slapped me on the back.

"Come home again, Carey. Meet my family. I've little ones."

"I'll be back," I grinned.

"Get in the car," Michelle Malone said.

We reboarded the Cessna Citation. They let me sit alone in the back of the plane, no longer under temporary arrest. I seemed to have passed the rigorous Mosley test of identity.

Somewhere over the Atlantic Hey-Zeus Rodriguez came back and sat down beside me. There was a sensation of emptiness, a barrier. He cleared his throat. "We had to check, Hawkins. The Employer ordered it. He has his ways and his ways become our ways. . . . You might know there were things about your background that just weren't clear."

"You still looking for Portales?"

"Someone will always be looking for your Señor Portales."

"You're just doing a job, right?"

Hey-Zeus pursed his lips and said: "After a fashion."

"Okay." I nodded. Then I added: "It's okay. I've worked for characters even more paranoid."

Hey-Zeus stiffened. "I don't like that word."

"You don't care for the word 'paranoid'? What word do you want? Name it and I'll use it."

Rodriguez wrinkled his brow, his dark eyes absorbing most curiously the artificial light from the reading lamp above the seat, then, rolling one of his muscled shoulders—the suggestion of a shrug—he whispered, "I'll forget you said it if you'll forget that I couldn't think of anything to replace it."

"You couldn't think."

"That's right. I'm under orders not to think. Serious orders." Hey-Zeus tapped his high forehead, precisely at the edge of his scalp.

He stared at me.

No, there was certainty—

As he broke the stare he slid from the seat. Standing in the narrow aisle, the tall Navaho reached into the front pocket of his turquoise Pendleton, pulled out a small package of unsalted peanuts (the package bearing the logo of Mosley Synoptics) and calmly popped a half dozen in his mouth. "Care for peanuts?" Hey-Zeus asked.

I didn't answer.

He went into the forward cabin with the pilots.

Seven

The night was too short, too compressed. The beeper began to bleat, an awkward fragment of alarm, a buzz.

Radiation dose, radium glow of a wristwatch: numbers solidified, numerals in green mist, disintegrating green mist. The sensation, bad sensation, had the flimsy steel of a dream, a dream with specifics, a dream with all the bolts and circuits and jargon, prism facets and fracture—

I woke. Coping, I saw that it was two A.M. and change. The beeper was going nuts. Video E-mail. I got out of bed, punched the computer, and the cursor expanded. The Seal of Mosley Synoptics appeared on the monitor screen, fading, followed by the face of Mosley, a grim face of Coleman Oswald Mosley, an unpackaged Mosley you won't see on *Larry King Live* or *Nightline*.

This contact, however, wasn't mail—it was a direct video telecom connection. The little CUCME computer TV camera above the computer monitor blinked on. Yeah, Coleman, *See You, See Me.* Now Mosley could *see* me, too.

Mosley snapped: "Hawk. New assignment. You and three others from the Bodyguard Detachment. You got a half hour to get your ass moving. It's Bosnia. Mosley Synoptics has agreed to do a little rescue work. Now don't tell me about the United Nations. Can't count on that rat's nest. Bosnia's a mess and the busybody U.N. messed things up even worse. Of course this is delicate, this assignment, very damn touchy, but when you can do someone a favor you do it. You follow me?"

I said I followed him. Mosley smiled—rather, his virtual figment on the computer smiled—and he said a short briefing file would give me the juicy details. His face faded.

An instant later the computer flashed a map of the Balkans, from Romania and Hungary down to Turkish Thrace and the straits. After a pan to disintegrated Yugoslavia (outlines of Serbia and Montenegro, a short focus on the bleeding hodgepodge of Bosnia, an elbow of Croatia) the granularity and magnification rapidly increased. The village of Zyconitza appeared. The name faded and a high-resolution satellite photograph filled the screen. The computer enhanced the satellite shot, delineating the gray stone house behind the line of conifers. Suddenly the two-dimensional photograph tilted and a three-dimensional, virtual projection of the stone house appeared, a light blinking in the third window of the second floor. Our objective was being held on the top floor, an androgynous voice said.

And then the details began, details of frightening

specificity, the circuits, bolts, bullets, and jargon. Our objective and our mission: Rescue Muhammad Samir al-Sahin, the son of a prince in one of the more obscure but wealthy United Arab Emirates. The rambunctious young man had picked up a scimitar (a Steyr AUG 5.56-millimeter assault rifle, actually) and gone to fight for Islam in Bosnia, to defend the Bosnian Muslims from Serbian-directed genocide. Young al-Sahin fancied himself one of the mujahideen, a holy warrior cut from the hard cloth of Afghanistan. Unfortunately, a clan of Bosnian Serbs (a clan that had been involved in the drug and cigarette smuggling trade before becoming holy Serbian Orthodox warriors) had captured the rich young ruler (who was a bit of a dandy, cut from cloth you find on the sidewalks of London Soho or in Picadilly Circus) and—the cruelest cut of all—the Serbs had sent a certifiable young al-Sahin toe to the boy's father. A demand note accompanied the toe, a demand note for several tens of millions of dollars.

I stared at a recent picture of the kid. The spoiled brat should have kept his rich oil ass at Cambridge and continued his studies in Sanskrit.

The computer flashed potential Drop Zones (DZs) and Landing Zones (LZs) in the Zyconitza area, potential avenues of ingress to the house. Avenues of egress appeared. Interior computer reconstructions of the house came next, the floor plan emerging in two dimensions, then transposing on the screen into crisp three-dimensional detail. I pressed a computer key and began a virtual-reality walk through the farmhouse. I was particularly interested in detailed lines of sight from the kitchen windows across the meadow, from the hallway leading to the staircase, and from the doorway of the upstairs bedroom into the upstairs hallway.

I reviewed short dossiers that had been compiled on the Serbs holding young al-Sahin. The men were killers. But they were not professional soldiers. As monsters went I had faced much worse. And Chatt had said to follow Mosley's orders.

I drew an MP5 sub with silencer and laser aiming device from the Mosley Synoptics weapons arsenal. The laser puts a pulse of light on the target, visible by the unaided eye out to one hundred meters. The laser site was calibrated for nine-millimeter subsonic ammunition. With the silencer and subsonic ammunition, a single report of the MP5 machine pistol would be scarcely as loud as a hardcover book falling from a desk and hitting the carpet. I was issued a set of night vision goggles, binocular lenses that amplify starlight or limited ambient light so that one can see at night with eighty percent of the clarity of day. I was issued a radio receiver that attached to my bush hat and a headset communicator, a highly miniaturized walkie-talkie that has a range of almost seven hundred meters. I was issued a hand-held thermal surveillance imager, a palmsized cameralike device that detects heat radiation the eye cannot. At three hundred meters it can detect a man lying beneath a bush and distinguish his heat signature from that of a deer. I was also issued a portable laser "dazzler," a weapon that fires a laser light burst that "blinds" night vision devices (like starlight scopes), observation devices (like binoculars), and weapons optics. The maximum range on the portable dazzler is some four hundred meters. At maximum power the weapon can fire one two-second laser light burst. The batteries are drained, but enemy optics caught in the swath of light are rendered useless for several minutes. The television screens of starlight scopes turn into a milky green haze, then go blank. Sometimes the optics are destroyed. A man looking through a pair of binoculars with nonfiltered lenses may be permanently blinded.

I lugged my weapons from the arsenal. Garcia and two other men, one named Blake and the other Louis, were waiting in the jeep that took us to the flight line. A fifth member of the team, a man named Pollock, was already on the ground in Zyconitza. Pollock was observing the farmhouse, using both visual and electronic surveillance equipment.

Garcia, Blake, Louis, and I spent the first three hours of the flight rehearsing the operation on the computers. We also made contact with Pollock via secure satellite phone.

Our intelligence was up-to-the-minute, what the general and admirals call real-time intelligence. Acoustic and thermal sensors Pollock had placed around the farmhouse gave us excellent data about movement and positions of guards. We also had other tactical advantages. The weather in the Zyconitza area was wet and rotten, in other words, perfect weather for a commando strike. With the rough mountain and forest terrain, the fog scraping the ground and the intermittent rain, our chances for achieving surprise increased dramatically. Fog and rain trick the eyes and shuffle the senses.

We had a psychological advantage as well. United

Nations relief helicopters landed infrequently near a Bosnian Muslim village located eight kilometers to the north of the farmhouse, so helicopters making a racket were no distinct cause for alarm. Serb artillery (122- and 130-millimeter, as well as 120-millimeter heavy mortars) were working over the Muslim city of Gorzabde, some thirty kilometers west. The kidnappers guarding the Arab prince would be used to disturbing noises in the distance.

The current state of negotiations also increased the opportunity for surprise. The young man's father had promised to pay the kidnappers forty million dollars. So they had been drinking. They were heady. They anticipated victory. They were getting lax.

An analysis of the Serbs' defensive preparations (aided by a recent satellite photograph) showed we were dealing with advanced amateurs. The sentry positions on the timbered ridge behind the farmhouse were actually rather well sited, one overlooking a meadow (which was clearly a potential helicopter landing zone), the other commanding the ridge and all rear approaches. Both were simple sandbag-and-rock emplacements, with a tarp raised on poles as a weak attempt to keep the rain from soaking the sentry on duty. Both positions had field telephones running back to the house. Pollock reported that one of the sentry positions, the one observing the meadow, had an SA-7B "Strella" shoulder-fired anti-aircraft missile sitting inside of it. Pollock had already made certain that the missile would not work. When the fifteen-year-old sentry on duty had fallen asleep (sleep aided by vast amounts of brandy), Pollock had crawled into the emplacement. He had opened the missile's shipping case and disabled its trigger housing. He had then closed the case.

There were usually ten guards inside the farmhouse. One was at the back door, one by the window in front, one in the upstairs hallway, and two inside the upstairs bedroom with the prince. The other five were "off-duty." They had beds in the basement of the farmhouse. The basement posed something of a problem. It had a reinforced concrete roof and firing slits covering all four sides of the farmhouse. All of the guards had walkie-talkies. Three other guards were sitting inside a BRDM armored car that was posted near a stone wall about five hundred meters down the road on the other side of the farmhouse. We were not particularly concerned about the armored car. We could deal with the armor if it became a problem.

The Citation landed at an airfield in Italy, near the coast south of Venice. We left the aircraft, stretched, then went to get some sleep in a Winnebago parked at the end of the airstrip. A helicopter would pick us up later that evening.

Nine P.M. local time (2100 hours). A young, black-haired woman woke us up. She wore a pistol in a holster slung over her left breast. We ate a high-caloric meal, then went out to the airfield. An L-100, the civilian version of a C-130 military cargo plane, was waiting for us.

Ninety minutes later we landed at an airstrip in

Bosnia. We transferred to the helicopter. The chopper was a UH-60 Black Hawk, a transport helicopter modified with long-range fuel tanks and upgraded electronics. The UH-60 also had launch racks carrying four Hellfire laser-guided missiles. M-60 light machine guns with drapes of linked ball ammunition hung on weapons pintles in the open doors.

The two pilots and the single air crew chief were Mosley Synoptics personnel. I recognized them.

Thirty minutes later the helicopter landed in a field behind the burned-out hulk of a building. We disembarked. A small pickup truck waited at the edge of the field. The truck's engine started and it rolled toward the aircraft. The chopper had to top off its fuel tanks and it would take about fifteen minutes.

Artillery, an erratic drum, slammed the distant mountains. Serbs were shelling Gorzabde. With each intermittent flash the night horizon fractured and cracked, the intervening moments of darkness a hasty black plaster.

We walked toward the burned-out building. Three days before, the ruins had been a mosque. Beside a skeletal minaret we ran an equipment check, all of us firing rounds from our weapons, all of us checking our radios and headsets, all of us once more turning on our night vision goggles, checking our thermal imagers, checking and rechecking our tie-downs.

Human bodies lay in the ruins of the mosque. In the eerie emerald green glow of the night vision goggles the corpses looked more like shocked contortions of brittle lava. The thermal imagers revealed hidden embers, beneath charred beams, in grotesque crannies, still smoldering amid the mosque's remains.

I gave the night vision goggles one further checkout. I maxed the power. The night was green kindling, ready to blaze in the electrified, amplified eyes of the goggles. As I adjusted the power I heard a movement. I turned. A topaz rabbit, or perhaps an emerald cat, fled from the stiff white husk of the mosque. With a flick I shut the goggles off.

The others finished their equipment checks. Garcia lit a cigarette. Tension made his face seem that much leaner.

"Let's go over the plan again, guys," Garcia said.

Our plan was quick and simple, as most good and successful military plans are in basic conception. At 4:00 A.M. local time a helicopter would put us and our equipment (including mountain bicycles) down in a field about ten kilometers south of the farmhouse. From there we would ride the wide-tired bikes to within three kilometers of the farmhouse. We would cache the bikes, then move on foot to hide positions below the timbered ridge.

The kidnappers changed sentries around 5:15 every morning. Their procedure was to make a radio or telephone call to the sentry post, then the two reliefs would leave the farmhouse and hike to the emplacements. They usually carried flashlights. As I said, the kidnappers made good smugglers, but they were poor soldiers. The morning replacements were supposed to call the farmhouse headquarters as soon as the night shift sentries left the position. The sentries were very lax about the security procedure, however. They often neglected to notify the farmhouse.

We planned on killing the relief guards, simultaneously taking out the sentries in the observation posts. We would use our silenced submachine guns or knives. Pollock also had a crossbow. Once the first four men were eliminated, I would then low-crawl over the lip of the ridge and down a fence line into the fallow field behind the farmhouse. At the edge of the field the kidnappers had rigged two clay-more mines. The mines were command detonated; that is, a buried electric line ran from the mines to the house. A soldier inside the house could press an electric detonator and fire the mines. One mine was sited to fire down the trail toward the sentry posts, the other to rake the yard behind the farmhouse.

I was to disarm the mines. On board the Citation I had rehearsed the claymore mine disarming proce-dure using a virtual-reality model on the computer and a training model of the mine. I know how to emplace and disarm mines, but there is no substitute for prac-tice, especially with claymores. Claymores are direc-tional mines; when they detonate the explosion is aimed in one particular direction. Essentially blocks of plastic explosive, when triggered the mines fire sev-eral hundred pellets in a fan, much like an immense shotgun.

Once I had disarmed the mines I would take a position behind an old well. At that point Pollock would try to get one last fix on where individuals were located inside the farmhouse, using the sensor sys-tem.

Garcia and Louis, wearing the hats and overcoats of the returning sentries, would then walk toward the back door of the farmhouse. We knew the kidnappers observed the returning guards through a primitive light-amplification night vision device. The kidnappers knew that this was a moment of particular vulnerability. As Garcia and Louis approached the farmhouse (with their backs toward me) I would shoot a beam from the laser dazzler. As I fired they would rush the house, kill the guard at the door, then dash upstairs.

Blake and I were to follow. Blake would fire a rifle grenade into one of the gun slits of the basement, either stunning or killing anyone in the underground bunker. I would head upstairs. Pollock would watch our rear.

We would finish our business with the Serbian guards, retrieve the prince, and head for the meadow. The helicopter would extract us.

If all went well we would be on the ground in Bosnia less than three hours. The success or failure of the operation would be decided in the first three seconds of assault.

We left the ruins of the mosque, returned to the helicopter, and took off.

Thirty minutes later, after weaving through stream-cut valleys and dancing along the shoulders of jagged Balkan mountains, the helicopter settled in a field. The mountain bicycles came out of the aircraft.

We moved like fast ghosts through the conifers and wet Balkan air.

We stashed the bicycles and linked up with Pollock. At 5:16 A.M. we killed the sentries and machine-gunned their relief, the quiet pop of the silencers lost in the rising wind, the bodies of the relief collapsing in the mist. Garcia and Louis made sure the sentries were dead. They also recovered the sentries' walkie-talkies. I crawled down the ridge, located the claymore mines, and disarmed them.

That's when the first mistake occurred.

War plans never go perfectly. Friction, there is always friction, hidden talons, fractal chaos that retards, slows, punctures. At some point in war, intelligence—what you think you know—always breaks down. Despite the thermal scans, despite the acoustic sensors, despite the satellite photos and pinpoint analysis, we had missed the stupid dog.

He must have been sleeping in the culvert behind the abandoned well. The mutt's sudden bark was dry. He sprang out of the culvert with a flash of teeth and I rolled away from his snap. He bit at my hand. I pressed the machine pistol barrel against his side and jerked the trigger. The bullet pierced his side. With a crapping howl he scampered up the ridge.

The guard in the doorway stepped out and hollered. He shined a halogen beam toward the field. The bright flashlight dazzled my night vision lenses. I quickly turned them off.

"What happened?" Garcia screamed over the radio.

"Dog!" I whispered.

The guard passed the light over my head. He called the dog's name. After no response he called again.

"It's dead now," a voice said over the radio. It sounded like Pollock.

The light beam played over the field. Then the guard switched it off. With a click I turned my night goggles back on.

"What's the call?" Louis asked over the radio.

"Wait," Garcia replied.

I hugged the wet ground, my cheek against a cold stone.

Then Garcia said: "There's a dude in the basement. At the gun slit to the right of the rear door. He has a starlight scope and it's on. Stay put, Hawk."

A moment later Pollock said: "No one else is moving. Looks like the dog didn't stir it up too long. If we're going we'd better move. When the guards don't show they'll get spooked."

"Go," Garcia whispered into his transmitter.

I sucked in a breath and quickly low-crawled from the edge of the field to the abandoned well. A cool sweat formed in my hair. Pulling the dazzler off of my back, I screwed the battery into the battery housing and flipped the power switch. The dazzler started to hum. It would take one minute for the power to maximize. The hum began to change into a potent, controlled whine.

The cool sweat began to snake from my hair, coiling in the rolled edge of my knit commando hat. The guard at the door once more stepped outside, a hard step. He snapped a couple of words into his walkie-talkie. I heard enough to know he was getting worried. He also sounded drunk. He flipped the flashlight on once more, shining the beam up the path toward the unseen sentry posts.

The soldier at the basement gun slit cursed. The flashlight went off. I upped the power on my night vision goggles. I could see the man in the basement bunker gun slit. He had his green-white hands up on the parapet. He wasn't using a starlight scope.

"Move now," I said into my mike. "They're not using night observation equipment. I can get a shot at the man in the gun slit."

Garcia made the decision. "Do it."

I dropped the dazzler and raised my MP5, snapping out the retractable shoulder stock. I switched the selector switch on my machine pistol from single shot to three-round burst. The laser range finder put a small red ball on the center of the head of the man standing at the gun slit. I fired. The rounds hit target. I moved to the guard at the door, the ball of laser light on his chest, and fired. He slammed backward on the stone porch, into the door. I put a second burst into his back. His knees jerked.

At that second Garcia and Louis ran through the open door. I flipped the selector switch to full automatic and raced after them, glancing back to check on Blake. I saw the large bulb of the rifle grenade he would fire into the bunker.

Garcia had blasted the light in the kitchen, so I kept my night vision goggles on as I kicked through the kitchen to the bunker stairwell. A sleepy man with an AK tumbled up the staircase from the basement. I fired a burst and he fell backward, arms out wide and crucified. As he fell the bunker beneath the house exploded and I dived sideways into the hall beside the main staircase, landing beside the body of the Serb who had been guarding the front of the house.

"Get here—" someone screamed over the radio, and I heard a blast, a heavy shotgun, and a scream. I slid my night vision goggles back on my forehead, stood, then bounded up the main staircase, hurdling the sprawled body of the guard the assault team had killed at the top of the stairs.

"Help me," Garcia screamed.

The Arab prince was screaming hysterically.

The two guards were dead, one next to a splintered straight-backed chair, the other in a sudden puddle on the floor.

The girl had a round in her shoulder and one in her gut. She lay doubled up on the floor. She slumped forward, blood running out of another hole in the back of her head.

"She came out of the closet, man," Garcia said.

Louis lay face forward on the floor. I rolled him over. His face was missing a chin.

"The chains," Garcia snapped. The chains and clamps binding the prince's legs to the floor were carbon steel. Garcia put his cutters around the chain right at the clamp. With a wrench the chain broke.

"Calm down," I said in Arabic.

The prince was babbling in Arabic, English, and French.

"Calm down," I said again.

Garcia broke the second chain. "Get Louis," Garcia said.

I put Louis's lifeless body on my back.

Garcia hustled the prince downstairs.

The building was starting to smolder. Blake had followed the fragmentation grenade with a thermite grenade. He was on his knee by the back door. He had his night vision goggles kicked back on his head.

"The dazzler," Garcia said.

"Got it," Blake replied.

I shifted Louis' weight and with a free hand brought my night vision goggles back over my eyes. We moved across the backyard, over the field, and toward the open meadow.

Pollock was on the radio, speaking to the helicopter crew. I couldn't tell if I heard my heart or if that was the thrum of chopper blades.

The Black Hawk popped up at the tree line.

"C'mon in," Garcia screamed.

But the chopper pilot slid his aircraft over the meadow. The helicopter jockeyed sideways, the dark gray mass of the low clouds a rumpled roof above the spinning rotor.

I looked back. Sometime in the last chaotic minutes dawn had begun, a sunlight scarcely apparent in the drizzle, but sunlight enough to begin to cause the night vision goggles to blur.

Still, I saw the motion.

"Armored car," the pilot's voice cracked.

With a lurch the Hellfire missile left the launch rack, the ball of flame shocking my eyes. I dropped to one knee. A moment later I heard the explosion. I kicked the goggles back off my eyes and watched the flame curl skyward.

The pilot fired a second missile, this one into the farmhouse. The missile struck the second story and blew the roof into hot pieces, the house a sudden foam of orange flame and crackling violent smoke.

"Here we go," Garcia said, more to the prince than to me.

The helicopter hovered six inches over the

meadow, the crew chief slapping a seat belt onto the frightened Arab prince, Garcia helping me lift Louis's body on board. "Bicycles. We don't leave class equipment like that," Garcia barked into his personal microphone. The pilot nodded. Blake and Pollock were crossing the field, lugging five of the ultralight mountain bikes and the laser dazzler. "Toss 'em the tether," the pilot said. With a quick wrap Pollock snaked a nylon tow through the frames of the bikes and tied off the line with a snap ring. Blake pitched me the dazzler and I clambered onto the chopper and found a seat, snapping on the quick release. As the Black Hawk began to climb, Blake and Pollock sprang on board. I glanced out the door. The nylon line went taut as the helicopter gained altitude, the clutch of gray bikes at the end of the tether rising from the ground.

I looked at Garcia. He gave me the thumbs-up sign, glanced at Louis' body, then told the whining prince to shut his silly trap.

Eight

My beeper went off. I woke. I had been dreaming, dreaming from the perspective of a satellite, a point way out there and watching with cameras and sensors, watching the house, the ice, the moraine, until the dream gathered like a slow comet and began to accelerate, began to drill through the cold, to quicken and narrow to a telescopic sight. I blinked. *The man in the sight.* I was certain I was awake. I felt like I was inside ice, in a glacier, not inside the optics of a telescopic sight. There was the cold sweat, sweat like piss from a glacier. I tried to look at my watch, to raise my frozen arm. *This time—*

The beeper went off again. Yes, this time I was awake. Screw it, I thought. My watch read 3:12 A.M. I got up and went to the computer, watched The Great Seal of Mosley congeal.

Mosley's E-mail was short and sweet. "Got a courier job for you, Hawk," he said. "Get out to the airport. You'll be filled in on board the aircraft."

*   *   *

I had plenty of time for fill-in.

The Citation landed fifteen hours later at Thu Bai in Thailand. In 1967 the Air Force had based Thunderchiefs and Phantoms out of Thu Bai, jet fighter-bombers striking targets in Laos and North Vietnam.

"Where are you going, sir?" the razor-faced customs officer asked in the hot shed that served as his inspection station and passport control.

The man had manners. He did not stare at the large Zero Halliburton aluminum briefcase handcuffed to my right wrist.

"Around Thailand," I replied. I handed him my passport. I did not pass him a bribe. That had already been arranged.

"I must inspect your luggage," he said.

He inspected the nylon bag that held my shaving kit and change of clothes. He continued to ignore the black metal briefcase chained to my body.

He did not inspect my nylon jacket. I had a Smith & Wesson nine-millimeter semiautomatic pistol inside the jacket. I also had two spare magazines.

Per the computer instructions, a man identifying himself as Major Su met me on the other side of the barbed-wire gate.

The identification routine was cute. I gave him a small credit card–sized plastic computer file. He slipped it into his palm-sized computer. His dark eyes flashed and he nodded. He handed me a similar file. I slipped it into my computer. The alfanumeric code jibed.

The Land Rover trip north took only a half hour. The dirt airstrip was surrounded by jungle. Thai women stood in the shadows of the jungle edge, watching and chattering. Ten minutes later the King Air arrived. There were no markings on the twin-engined aircraft. The aircrew, like Major Su, were all Chinese. We flew north toward Chiang Mai and the highlands.

"Brandy?" Major Su asked when we were airborne.

I said no.

"You understand," Major Su said very seriously, "that General Lai prefers no one in Thu Bai know his private airplane is picking up an American guest. The Thai government gives the Kuomintang some leeway, if we are discreet."

I said I understood discretion.

I met the general in his backyard. He was sipping a gin and tonic. His head was bald, his black eyes tenacious. His military bearing put starch in the drab blue business suit.

"Follow me into the garden," General Lai said. I followed. Jade boulders formed sleek and blue-green wedges among the orchids and looping vines. The huge, smooth jade slabs poked from the black garden soil like nameless gravestones or teeth from a jewel Godzilla.

I said I was impressed by his rock collection.

General Lai shrugged. "The jade? Lovely and

expensive, yes. The gemstones do enchant this . . . this very well-secured garden. But it is a shame such exquisite jade must be concealed. The stones are museum quality, without compare. I feel something like a Bedouin who drapes his young wives with gold bracelets, then hides their bodies beneath despicable cloaks." His smile was taut and fleeting. "Regretfully I describe this garden as my bank account of last resort. So please sit." He pointed to a pair of chairs, turning his palm over with the same calculated elegance a Vegas dealer exhibits when exposing a winning ace.

I thought, for a moment, of Jessica's jade eyes, but the thought elapsed.

We sat in the wicker chairs next to a pool. White and orange fish swam beneath the glass surface, the white fish with skin like opals. The sky was clear and blue, yet even at this altitude the touch of humidity remained.

"You must open it," the general said. He did not smile.

"Yes." I opened the aluminum briefcase.

The tightly compressed bills smelled the green life-less smell of unpawed cash trucked straight from the Treasury. There were two hundred stacks of cash, each stack with an even hundred one-hundred-dollar bills. Two million dollars.

Now General Lai smiled with satisfaction. He yelled to one of his bodyguards who was waiting in a shadow. The guard hustled over, took the briefcase, and double-timed off through the garden. The General ordered tea for himself and for me. "Mint? You prefer hot mint tea? You know, we are a bit archaic. In this land, if a man has wealth, he buys gold or rubies." His eyes fixed on one of the huge jade boulders. "Or jade. You may tell Mr. Mosley that this down payment will assure him a new airport will be built. To his specifications."

I did not know what this payment was about, but I said: "I shall tell him." Then I added, guessing that Chatt would want to know, "Mr. Mosley is ready to use the airport as soon as it is built."

The General nodded. "Tell him I am ready for the legalization of drugs in America. You can remind him of my political proposal, legalization with stigmatization. Not a poetic phrase but appropriate. A good bumper sticker, I believe, small enough for anyone to grasp, opaque enough to mean what it needs to mean. Politics, like space and time, is curved. Here to there is never direct. Rhetoric gives the appearance of straight lines. The minions need the appearance of straight lines, in order to follow. Of all people on this earth Mosley understands these physics. Politics will open our market. And when it's done the air freighter field at Chiang Mai will be a ready asset. Assure Mr. Mosley of our intent to cooperate. Yes, I think I see our tea on its way through the flower garden."

And I understood the mission. Like General Lai, of the Fourth Kuomintang Army, the Chinese Nationalist forces that retreated out of Yunnan Province in 1950 and took up residence in the Golden Triangle of Thailand, Burma, and Laos, the renegade Chinese Army that became the first organized drug army in Southeast Asia, I understood the indirect approach.

"Tell Mr. Mosley I will be in touch," General Lai said as I left for his airfield.

I told him I would convey the message.

*   *   *

The next assignment came two days later. Instead of being asleep I was riding on the monorail line back from the mall when my beeper went off. I reported to the Security Detachment Two-Zero headquarters.

Garcia was already there. "We've already drawn equipment," he said. I thought he looked bushed.

"Bosnia again?" I joked.

"Shit. This makes The Boz look like cake. You'll get a briefing on board the aircraft."

The 747 Special Performance air freighter was loaded with sacks of USDA flour and rice. Beneath the sacks of food they stashed the tools: .50 caliber heavy machine guns and antitank guided missile launchers.

The 747 landed in Addis Ababa, Ethiopia. A forklift started unloading the sacked flour and rice. Three pallets were transferred to a familiar craft, a Lockheed L-100, and we followed the three pallets.

I've no idea where the dirt airstrip was located, it could have been in southeastern Ethiopia, it may have been Somalia. As the L-100 hit the strip the camels ran toward the thorn scrub.

We spent the night in a tent. The wind blew, flapping the tent incessantly. The next morning I shaved using an aluminum canteen cup as a washbasin. About noon a column of ten Land Rovers arrived and we spent the afternoon installing the heavy machine guns and antitank missile launchers on the vehicles.

The warlord was named Said Farah Hassan. He had been the number-two man in a southern Somali clan. His heavily armed technical vehicles had clashed with a U.N. column a couple of months back, but what put him on the United Nations most-wanted list was the assassination of the U.N. High Commissioner for Refugees. The patsy U.N. couldn't lay a hand on Said Hassan. "But Mosley Synoptics can, can't we?" Mosley said on the computer monitor Garcia had placed inside the tent and attached to a direct-link satellite dish. "Now, here's the latest intelligence we have been able to glean from our resources."

The intelligence was not complete, but Mosley said it was very reliable, very close. Said Hassan had fled across the border into Kenya and had holed up in a compound outside a small village. He had approximately thirty men around him, as well as family and retinue—eighty people, all told, including our reliable source.

Our logistics was the challenge. The next day the UH-60 Black Hawk arrived. The Black Hawk helicopter had already airlifted fuel bladders filled with gasoline, crates of ammunition, water bladders, and tear gas canisters to a site about fifteen kilometers from the village. What took the helicopter three hours one-way took us two days to traverse. The terrain starts off as gullied hell split by hot salt pans, then it starts to rise toward the arid plateaus. My Land Rover hit every rock, rut, and cranny on the trail.

We struck Said Hassan's compound before dawn. There were thirty-three of us in the ground assault group. Said's sentries were killed with silenced machine pistols. Then, five hundred meters from the

compound, we fired a dozen of the huge six-liter tear
gas canisters. In the emerald world of night vision
goggles the rocket-propelled canisters rumbled toward
the mud-walled compound, tumbling like huge water-
melons spewing CS tear gas.

A TOW antitank missile spit from its launcher and
the thick wooden door securing the entrance to the
compound evaporated as the missile struck.

Eight of the Land Rovers then rushed the compound. We wore gas masks fitted with night vision
goggles. To the Somali tribesmen we must have
looked like alien lizards rising out of the desert,
spilling from the vehicles.

As we entered the compound the air assault party
arrived, six men rappelling down from the helicopter
hovering above the galvanized tin palace of Said
Farah Hassan.

Inside the compound men and women screamed
and retched, the tear gas completely disrupting the
tribesmen. Garcia and I both shot two armed men as
they fell coughing out of the first floor of the tin-sided
building. A third, a man wearing a Chicago Cubs
baseball cap, died on the staircase, his body absorbing
an orange stream of tracers. He toppled at my feet
and the brim of his cap caught the toe of my boot. It
was as if I were in a very precise nightmare.

Over my radio I heard the announcement: "We've
got him. We've got him."

I ran up the staircase. Outside, over a loudspeaker
on one of the Land Rovers, a Mosley Synoptics lin-
guist told the tribespeople, if they wanted to breathe,
to exit through the compound entrance. Exit in good
order, please.

Two Mosley Synoptic bodyguards (both from the air assault party) were hauling a very sleepy-looking (yet coughing and retching, which was a trick) little man down the hallway. He wobbled, his knees spine-less nylon. But then Said Farah Hassan had been slipped more than his share of sleeping pills.

"Where?" I asked.

"First room, Hawk," was the reply. "Watch the glass."

The room was chaos. The dead Somali on the floor had been shot in the head.

I saw her.

She had her elegance, she would always have that physical dignity.

Sari stood over the body, sucking fresh air from an oxygen-fed gas mask. She coughed, the cough muffled by the rubber mask and canister. She shivered, and her tall and distorted reflection in the cracked dressing mirror on the wall shivered in fragments, her surface further detached from self, a mosaic of a woman. Another suck of oxygen and she turned, her head—in that shattered reflection—absorbed to the neck by the alien insect bubble of the gas mask, its convoluted tubes and olive drab sheath.

"Your work?" I asked, pointing to the dead Somali guard. I touched the shatter of his head with the toe of my boot. "Sari? Hey. It's me." I moved near her.

I could see her eyes through the broad, eerie lenses of the gas mask. Her eyes were tears, streams from brown pools. She mumbled something through the gas mask's speaker port and I told her I couldn't hear her, couldn't at all.

She ripped the mask away from her face. "Yes," she hissed, the tears spilling. "My terrible work."

She gagged on the gas. Her body heaved.

"Keep the mask on," I said. I pushed the mask back onto her face.

A spasm of shivers wracked her.

"Carey," she said. I heard her say my name clearly. "My work," she said again. The missing word wasn't missing. *Terrible.* I could feel her body choke on the word *terrible,* like her brain and heart and guts were trying to strangle it. Terrible deceit.

Another sob shook her body. I helped her clear the mask and get a good tight fit. "Suck oxygen, then blow the gas out. Blow. Do it. Blow, damn it. That's right."

She managed. Once she began to cope I put my arm around her and led her down the staircase.

Nine

Mosley's next move was swift. He did not give me time to decompress from combat, to shed the pressure of violence. He did not give me time to regain my balance.

As I left the Citation business jet I saw Hey-Zeus Rodriguez and Michelle Malone standing beside a jeep parked on the runway apron. Malone had an MP-5 submachine gun slung over her shoulder. She was biting her lip, a nervous shark too hungry to wait for the bait.

Rodriguez yelled something, but the yell disappeared in the jet whine of revving air freighter engines. In the garish night lights the huge 747 passed behind them like a bulbous gray-white whale. Rodriguez scowled, pointed at me, then pointed at the jeep. I got the message. Lugging my kit, I walked across the runway to the apron.

"Still got camouflage stick on your face," Rodriguez observed. "You look beat. Is that desert sand I smell? The Sahara has a smell to it, doesn't it? How was the flight from Cairo?"

"Weary."

"Better suck it up and get your shit together," Michelle Malone frowned. "The Employer wants you to fly out with him at three A.M."

I looked at Rodriguez. His black eyes told me zero. The crystal pendant lying in the break of his denim jacket told me zero. So I looked at my watch. It was 10:00 P.M. local time, in The Area. That made it around 6:00 A.M. tomorrow, Sudanese time. My body clock was still airborne. "I need some rest," I said.

"That's not the right response," Malone snapped. "The right response is 'Where to, Mr. Mosley?'"

"All right. Where to?"

"Get in the jeep," she replied.

I showered. At 11:00 P.M. a barber showed up at my apartment. He took a little off the sides and the top. At midnight two tailors showed up. They fitted me for a business suit. The three-piece suit arrived at 2:00 A.M. The suit coat and pants were blue wool and very Brooks Brothers. The vest, the third piece, which blended perfectly with the suit, was an ultralight Kevlar and semi-dyne. "Our lightest bulletproof," the older tailor said with a nod. "Should stop a nine millimeter short or .380 ACP cold if range is over five meters. So run from a gun," he winked.

I spent the next few minutes reflecting. I thought of Courtney. I closed my eyes, focused, saw my daughter's smile and heard her laugh. I fixed a mental image, a string of images, a mental movie of sign language, our hand sign encryption for the words "I love you." Then I cleared my mind. I felt refreshed. I hoped Barb Angleton and Fazzari were doing exactly what they had been trained to do.

At 2:45 A.M. Hey-Zeus Rodriguez and an armorer arrived. The armorer gave me a Walther PPK/S and a shoulder holster.

Hey-Zeus drove me to the flight line in his silver Jaguar. "You're flying with Mosley," Hey-Zeus said as we left the Two-Zero building parking lot. "On his bird."

"I read the E-mail," I replied.

As we drove past the loading docks it became another moment when you simply decide.

"Hey-Zeus . . . I've noticed that pendant you wear. The crystal. It's unusual."

He glanced at me. "You mean my beads and trinket?"

"Yes."

"Catches your eye, huh? Think you make trade with Injun? Sorry, Hawkins. I wouldn't trade it for Manhattan." His glance became a stare.

I waited. I waited carefully. But I felt no anticipation, no radiation, no inkling, and that disturbed me. It had been days since I had had an expectation, days since I had had a sense of Chatterley. I suppose that's why the crystal attracted me, for the crystal had the facets of Prism. My mind wanted to dive into its planes and surfaces, for a brief moment to escape not just The Area but this constricting universe. Of course I can soldier in isolation, I can go on for years in a hellhole, fulfilling the mission. But this new mission, what Mosley had carved out of the approaching morning—I admitted I desperately wanted direction, I wanted insight, I wanted Chatterley inside my mind. I

wanted her to tell me what to expect, how to react,
how she wanted me to handle incidents and emotions
that I knew would be, emotions that can shatter the
strongest crystal, that could break me and—yes, I
knew this to be damn well the case—emotions which
could test even her most able psychic talent.

"Hawkins? You all right?" Hey-Zeus asked.

"Huh? Yeah. Sure."

"Tired?"

"Yeah. I'm whipped."

He turned the steering wheel.

"We're here," Hey-Zeus said a moment later as the
Jaguar stopped beside the aircraft ramp. As I climbed
out of the car he called: "Hey, Hawk. Have fun in
Washington. And don't paint the White House red."

We entered the White House through the West Wing.
"Wunnerful. Wunnerful," Coleman Mosley said as the
Marine corporal snapped to attention. The only press
up at 6:15 A.M. was a white-haired relic with a spiral
notepad, a pencil, and a steaming cup of coffee. The
old reporter tried to ask Mosley why a surprise, unan-
nounced visit with the president? Did it have anything
to do with the alleged capture of Said Farah Hassan?
Mosley's response was a clipped "Good God, Nelson.
What have you been smoking? To dream up a question like that."

"You're not going to answer my question?"
Howard Nelson asked.

"Friend, I'm going to have one of my people send
you a pocketbook computer," Mosley winked. "It'll
improve your productivity."

We left the lone reporter in the anteroom as two Secret Service men, both with crew cuts and flat brown eyes, escorted us down the hall.

"Who let the press in?" Mosley fumed.

The Secret Service men were too smart to reply.

"Who let the press in?" Mosley repeated as we met Garner, the Secret Service chief.

Garner scowled and ignored the question. He nodded at me. "You can't bring your own armed bodyguard in, Mosley, you know the rules."

"I got my bodyguard and Duncan's got his," Mosley smiled.

"Sir, you're no head of state."

"Mr. Garner," Mosley said, his smile broadening. "Now you're an old friend of my friend Colonel Ray Garcia, isn't that right? Of course that's right. And you know damn well there's a conspiracy to kill me. Everyone knows it. Now last night I asked ol' Ray, Could the Secret Service do it? And by do it I mean kill me. And Ray said, Of course they could, Mr. Mosley. Or Duncan himself could do it. I said to Ray, That sounds almost traitorous, telling me the president could assassinate me. Why, if I didn't know you, Ray, I'd say it was traitorous, a traitorous thought. But you know Ray, don't you, Mr. Garner?"

Mosley twirled a long handlebar as if trying to wring the red from his mustache. "But Ray said, Mr. Mosley, you asked. And Duncan could kill you. Or for that matter . . ." Mosley said, his eyebrows rising as he peered down the hall at an approaching figure, "his wife."

*   *   *

The first lady came straight up to Mosley. "Let the bodyguard in," she said to Garner. "But no weapons. We're against weapons."

She flashed a wide, winning smile. But I did not look at her. I could barely glance at Mrs. Duncan, at her eyes. I put my hesitant stare on the taut crimson bow she wore on her blue woman's business suit. I wanted her to leave. I expected her to leave. That expectation made me feel confident.

But, after Garner took my PPK/S and my knife, Mrs. Duncan turned and faced me directly, smiling a wide and professional smile. "And what is your name?" she asked with a lilt. She balanced perkily on her blue pumps.

"Hawkins," I said.

"You've real steel in your eye, Hawkins, did you know that?" She stuck out her right hand. "Hi. I'm Carolyn Duncan."

"Delighted," I said, surprised at my own smoothness.

Her hand was firm, warm, delicate at the fingertips.

"You seem to be an early morning type, Mr. Hawkins, all ready to face the trials of daylight."

"I like to think I'm particularly fine in the morning."

Mrs. Duncan giggled. "Well. My son Hardin is a morning person, a very morning person . . . not surprising, I suppose." Her eyes were wide and deep. I turned my head away. Her eyes were deep mirrors. She giggled again. It was a bright, graceful giggle, but a giggle with a secret, the laugh of a woman bemused at a private joke beyond the comprehension of awkward beefcake Secret Service men standing in the hallway.

Suddenly she reached out and put her hand on my

shoulder. I started to cringe. "There's no reason to cringe," she laughed. It was a friendly laugh. "I'm not poison. Despite what the press and my detractors say I can be quite charming. Now . . . you seem very fit. I like mountain bikes. Do you work out a lot?"

"I am fit," I replied.

"Hey. Get this Spartan a glazed doughnut," she said with a chuckle. "Or do you prefer powdered?"

"I'll pass on the doughnut."

She cocked a blonde eyebrow. "Irritated that I'd test your discipline, Hawkins? But why shouldn't I? I understand Mosley is a man who appreciates the disciplined."

I wanted to reply, to reply accurately, knowing that witty replies aren't one of my strengths. This time, however, I didn't have to reply. "Hey—Carolyn?" the president called from inside the Oval Office. "Is that you? C'mon in here." Duncan, wearing a gray jogging suit and a Ford gimme cap, stood in front of his desk. Mosley was already seated. Mosley motioned with his hand, a vague swat at the heavy air.

I started to march through the doorway.

But Mrs. Duncan put her firm palm on the center of my chest. I flinched. Even through the plastic armor of the bulletproof vest the touch lingered long enough for my heart to feel it.

She pulled her hand away, though the palm's impression lingered. "Stay here, Hawkins," she said crisply. "You stay out here as well, Garner," she nodded. "And that's an order."

"Yes ma'am."

Without looking into the room where her husband faced Mosley, Mrs. Duncan closed the door, and, so quietly, her tread scarcely impressing the deep carpet, she walked down the hallway toward a narrow stair-case.

Trying to fake casual, and failing, I waited in the hall-way with the Secret Service. I refused the doughnut—a glazed doughnut—when it arrived, but requested a cup of tea, hot mint preferably. "We've some mint tea brewed," the steward nodded.

"Really?"

"Put on the menu this morning. Shall I get you a pot?"

"No . . . mint, huh . . . get me just one cup. That'll do fine."

The waiting was not easy. Of course it wasn't going to be easy for me. But I could feel the strain in Garner, in the other Secret Service men. Then I real-ized I felt more than strain. I could feel an expectant tension. The tension had form. I started to resist, then I gave up and did not try to block it out.

The tea came. I killed the cup in two long draughts.

As I gave the steward the empty cup we heard President Randall Duncan raise his voice. "Damn you—" Duncan began. Then Mosley shouted. Duncan shouted. And there was another curse. Then silence followed, the kind of silence that drills a hole in time.

"Man," Garner said, shaking his head. He stopped. The pulse at his temple stiffened. I knew he wanted to say something else but the Secret Service knows how to keep silent.

I gazed at him. Garner tried to gaze back, but he

looked away. With a shake of his head his eyes dropped to the floor and his cool demeanor fell as well. "Crap," he whispered. "What crap. Any more of this and my gut will be nothin' but a bucket of acid."

"This kind of argument happen much?" I asked.

"This must be your first time here, huh."

I caught the glint in his eye. His guard was going back up. Could I, should I, here in the White House, attempt a probe without a prism? I felt no sense of anticipation, none at all. The tension had eased. I resisted but—how does one describe this?—I visualized, or it made itself real, so real, crystal, moving darkness in a moment so mundane. Gazing at him I asked: "Do Mosley and Duncan meet often?"

Garner scowled. I tried to probe. Yeah, to hell with Chatt's orders. I decided to see how far I could go, right there, *only for a second*. It was no rebellion. It was an operational demand. Was I able to use the change? *Getting more able*. The probe didn't work, not well. It was goddamned opaque, no clarity, no dead certainties. But the Garner probe was instructive. I could sense the balancing act in his mind—my ableness inside—one thought, another, Garner's rapid shifts between choice of professional silence or intimate trust. *One can affect the balance, can't one, Chatterley? Tip the unable subject's balance, a step from suggesting, two steps from directing . . .*

Something clicked.

"C'mon, man, I'm not the press," I said with a shrug.

Garner bit his lip. "Depends on which Duncan you mean by often. Your boss and the first lady have met several times . . ." He tensed again. In a coarse, flinty whisper he said: "Hawkins, I'm breaking the law standing out here with him out of my sight. Breaking my goddamn teeth. But that's the way Duncan likes to play it."

"Fast and loose, huh."

"No. Indifferent."

Shouts—our heads swerved simultaneously. "Ah tol' you—" Mosley screamed. Garner stiffened. He signaled the two other Secret Service agents in the hallway.

She must have walked on pillows and a cloak because none of us heard her or saw her until she reached the door.

"Mrs. Duncan," Garner began.

"Stay here and do nothing. Both of you. I'll handle this." With a quick twist Mrs. Duncan opened the door and entered the room. She didn't glance at either Garner or me. She didn't have to glance.

Garner folded his arms across his chest. "She'll make peace or break them apart."

Mosley started shouting again. All three Secret Service men tensed. I tensed. I wanted guidance but there was only emptiness, no crystal, just a confusion of voices and inability.

"Hey, Chief," one of the Secret Service men growled to Garner. "You know the score. We have to protect him."

That seemed to be the spark Garner needed. "Come on," Garner barked. His fist balled. Quick rush and the Secret Service men burst into the Oval Office. I followed.

And we froze. The tableau was confusing. Garner and his men stood there, flustered. The fluster turned to embarrassment.

"Well I'll be," President Duncan said.

The red-faced President Duncan stood by a chart on a chart frame. The red-faced Mosley was sitting in a chair, seated like a human pretzel with legs tightly crossed, arms X'ed across his chest. The first lady pointed a direct, elegant finger at both of the men.

"Mr. President," Garner said. "We got worried when—"

"I'm just fine," Duncan said.

Garner looked at Mosley then at Mrs. Duncan.

"I said I'm fine, Mr. Garner," Duncan nodded.

Garner took a step toward Mosley. I stepped toward Garner.

"Stop. Right there," Mrs. Duncan said. Garner and I stopped. "Now . . . my husband says he's fine. So you may get out," Mrs. Duncan continued, casting another cool glance at Garner. "And when I say I'll handle it I will."

"I have a job, Mrs. Duncan."

"And you do a good job," she replied, flashing a charming smile. "A *dignified* job. So relax. And get dignified." The smile and the look from her eyes appeared to catch Garner exactly right, to catch him perfectly. I also felt more relaxed, without sensation.

"Yes, ma'am," Garner muttered. "I'm . . . I'm sorry."

The Secret Service men trooped past me.

"Now Cole—" Duncan began.

"Blather. You're all blather," Mosley interrupted.

"You requested this meeting," Duncan said with a surge of anger. "I found time."

"You requested this meeting," Mosley retorted, "and I damn well showed."

Garner stopped at the doorway.

The first lady looked at the president and Coleman Mosley.

"I set the meeting," the first lady said. "This disagreement will be settled. It must be settled. The penalty for quitting's damnably heavy. Do you understand?"

Could she settle it?

Yes, when will it settle?

I went through the door. There was a tug as I left, perceptible, but I could not bring myself to look back at her, to look over my shoulder, to cast a quick glance at her blazing face.

Ten

We left the White House. The Marine corporal cracked off a salute. Mosley and I walked down the drive toward the waiting black Cadillac limousine, with the reporter, old Howard Nelson, tagging like a white-haired bloodhound who has the first tantalizing scent and now begins to separate the hot smell of trail from the stink of confusion.

I stopped beside the limo. For a moment I left my mind unguarded, accepting any impulse from Chatterley. I did feel an anticipation that I knew was not solely my own. So I acted. No, I did not use Prism. I put my new energy, my increasing ableness into the thought. *Chatterley. When does the charade end. Stop the toying. When do I move?* I waited. I waited for guidance.

I blinked and realized I was staring at Mosley.

Mosley, holding the rear door to the limousine, said in his soft twang: "Don't look so dazed, Hawk. It'll all work out." He slapped me on the back. "G'wan. Get in."

"What will work out, Mr. Mosley."

Mosley, his eyebrow arching, put his finger to his lips, then pointed at Nelson, Mosley's index finger suddenly a pistol barrel with a cocking thumb.

Howard Nelson, walking toward the limousine, dropped his head forward, his black glasses sliding down to the tip of his nose. Nelson stopped beside the car and considered Mosley's finger pistol. Then he returned fire: he pointed his pencil at Mosley's head.

Mosley grinned. As he slid into the rear seat the billionaire's pointing finger turned into a bye-bye wave of the hand. "We'll be gittin' you that computer, Howard. It'll hep you more than the New Deal ever did." Mosley started to close the car door.

Nelson grasped the door. "I didn't cover the New Deal, Coleman. I got my break in World War Two," Nelson replied, ". . . in combat."

Mosley's bald head was as smooth as glass and his eyes calm ice. "The World War Two," Mosley said. "So a hero like you shoulda been drawin' Social Security years ago, Howard. You needta retire to a nice fat PR job. You want me to arrange something?"

"I'll pass, Coleman."

"You're a little old for talking-head work, Howard, but makeup does wonders. CNN needs the geriatric point of view."

"What's with you and Duncan, Coleman."

"If we get you an afternoon time slot you won't have to be hanging around the White House at 6:00 A.M., so you won't look so fearsome weary."

Nelson flashed a smile. You could see the coffee stains on his teeth. The bloodhound kept pushing. "Why don't you fill me in on what you and the Duncans are chatting about these days?"

Mosley stiffened. "Ask Duncan. He's president. I'm not."

Nelson rapped his pencil on the side of the limo. "I've asked the White House why there was no release to the White House press corps about your *visits.*"

"Mebbe they wanted you to have a scoop. Who told you?"

"Nobody," Nelson replied.

"You psychic?" Mosley asked sarcastically.

"I've learned to feel bad weather in my bones and shit between my toes."

"Then it's time for you to learn to avoid manure and move on to greener pastures."

"Can I quote you? To the FBI?"

"Better them than your infected newspaper. Let go of the door."

Nelson's hand released. With a jerk Mosley pulled the door to the limo closed. "Let's git away from the press," Mosley snapped to the driver. "Pronto."

As we turned out of the drive onto Pennsylvania Avenue, Mosley said in a very clipped voice, "We've got a little ree-quest, Hawk."

"A request for what."

"From powerful folks who need a powerful favor."

Mosley left me at Dulles. He flew to God knows where. The Citation flew me to The Island.

The computer briefing I received on board the aircraft was three hours' worth of information about maritime terrorism and piracy. The initial material had all the charm and wit of any government-derived background study, the expected statistics, the mummified bureaucratic prose: "The U.S. depends on seaborne tanker transport for 85 percent of its petroleum imports, and while such tankers are potentially vulnerable, the threat to petroleum transport by sea from terrorist attacks appears to be low." The computer produced a series of charts highlighting U.S. dependence on foreign oil. Then: "More than sixty incidents of maritime terrorism of various types have occurred over the past fifteen years, but these constitute less than one percent of all international terrorist incidents during that time frame. Most terrorists have limited maritime capabilities and attacks involving maritime targets and/or tactics appear to be harder to carry out successfully than other types of terrorist attacks. Yet piracy (criminal attacks on ships on the high seas) has increased in recent years to an estimated 350 incidents within the last year. Contemporary piracy consists primarily of boarding ships by force or under cover of darkness, usually by armed men on speedboats, and theft of money or valuables from ships and crews. Thefts of cargo are less common. The highest-risk area for piracies is the Strait of Malacca, lying between Singapore and Indonesia, with 244 incidents recorded over the last eighteen-month period. The Strait is the heaviest traveled waterway in the world, with over 45,000 ship transits annually."

A great deal of information followed, discussing specific attacks in the Strait of Malacca, currents in the Strait of Malacca and the Singapore Strait (Phillip Channel, specifically), the patrol areas of the Malaysian, Indonesian, Singaporean, and U.S. navies in the Strait zone. The information package included a technical intelligence assessment analyzing attacks by unmanned ships (citing a Palestinian use of a radio-controlled boat to attack the Israeli port of Eilat, a sort of nautical car bomb) and the potential for unmanned ship attacks by various terrorist and criminal organizations, particularly in Asia.

Ray Garcia met me on the landing apron of The Island's airport. "Hey, Hawk," he said. "Get in the jeep. You and I are gonna start getting wet."

I first saw the minisubmarine the next morning. She was Russian-made, Garcia said. Designed for Soviet spetznaz special forces operators when they were still Soviets. "The latest and possibly the last of a minisub class well tested in the Baltic," Ray grinned. "Ask the Swedes what a teasing bitch it is to find these things." Eleven meters in length, she had the bulbous head of a killer whale, the bow quickly tapering into a long, fat cigar of black titanium, the small hump of a conning tower and hatch rising like a smoothly stunted dorsal fin.

"This babe's hot, Hawk. Diesel-electric propulsion with towed snorkel option and submerged diesel dash capability," Ray said. "She's got range. You know what that means? It means you don't need to suck up close to the mother ship." Ray said the stat sheet the Russians provided to Mosley said the ultrahushed diesel moved her at eighteen kilometers per hour with a radial range of operations (at that speed) of 175 kilometers. The electric motor moved her at a silent seven kilometers an hour for eight hours.

"And we brought in a couple of German diesel sub experts for modifications," Ray told me as we boarded the sub and I peered down the hatch. "Man, everything's now out on the market. She's now got some shit as fancy as the nuclear big boys." The modifications: Extensive acoustic tiles. Active and passive sonar arrays. An electronics and radar array co-located with the periscope. "And this mod's really nifty." Garcia pointed to a smooth metal swelling behind the nub of a conning tower. "Pop-up armored box launcher. Contains three surface-to-air missiles. Can't be more than two meters deep if you shoot but the antiaircraft missiles have self-targeting capability. They'll wax hell out of an antisub helicopter that's tailing you."

I clambered down the hatch.

The sub had the cool smell of a high-tech coffin.

She was an impressive coffin. She had dry space for six personnel as well as stowage for weapons and scuba and rebreather equipment. The bow had a broad glass observation port. The aquarium reversed: sunfish and an amberjack gazed into the bow window, their gills slowly pulsing at a dreamlike pace. In the middle of the chamber was a dive lock. Through the portholes I could see two underwater sleds riding inside the lock and the ventral hatch. There was one aft torpedo tube which fired a 250-millimeter acoustic torpedo of two meters in length or a small 200-millimeter cruise missile of similar length. There was stowage space on board for three of the torpedoes and two of the missiles.

Garcia followed me down. "Nice dive lock. You

can use the top hatch to launch divers singly or send a squad out the bottom. This sucker's a real SEAL's dream machine. Course, the U.S. Navy doesn't have one this state-of-the-art."

"Right," I said. "Rely on Mosley Synoptics."

We took the sub out that afternoon. We submerged and put up the snorkel. I maxed the diesels. We hit twenty-two kilometers an hour and sustained it for an hour. We pulled in the snorkel, shut off the diesel, and dived deeper, the sunlight bluing, greening, darkening as we entered the colder waters. I maxed the electric engine. For a blistering twenty minutes the sub made fourteen kilometers per hour, then the batteries began to lose power precipitously. We surfaced. Global positioning put us twenty-four kilometers south-southeast of The Island. With the sea calm Ray popped the hatch. A bright shaft of sunlight fell through the opening. Pulling a pair of sunglasses out of my sea vest, I followed Garcia out. The sky was a cloudless dome of blue-white, the sea a billiard surface of turquoise.

We sat there for a few moments, Garcia hunkering on the bow, staring into the blue water.

"Nice, huh, Hawk."

"You bet."

"Man. I don't want for nothing right now. Not a beer. Not even a fishing line. This. Simple this . . . you ever feel that way?"

"You bet."

The sea moved the craft so gently. The sun reflected a thousand diamonds off the water's shimmering surface, a thousand shifting prisms. I put on my sunglasses.

Garcia's beeper went off.

He cursed. "Of course. The Employer. Man, oh man. Lemme get to the damned computer." Garcia eased around me and went back down inside the sub.

The Employer. Mosley. What interested Mosley and Duncan in the Strait of Malacca? I once more began to consider several scenarios. I began to focus—

No. Enjoy simple this. I cleared my mind.

My cleared mind gazed across the becalmed, rippleless sea. And I looked up at the sun. It hung in the sky like a burning prism.

Sensations.

I ripped the sunglasses from my face and closed my eyes. I put energy into the thought. *Chatterley. What the hell am I supposed to do?* I waited. I opened my eyes. But the sun was only like a prism. It had no facets. The dazzling reflections were like diamonds. They had no depths. But—damn it all—in moments of death crisis or moments of peaceful living bliss the capable do not need objects, the able do not need a prism's focusing angles and planes. A moment of living bliss only darkened by doubt, doubt shading me from connecting consciousness. I tried again to force a channel. *Chatterley. What the hell am I supposed to do.* I waited, my entire mind an antenna. I no longer felt the sun, the slow roll of the sea. The moment focused, a channeled flood of the universe. *Chatterley. What occupies you? Why have you toyed with me? Damn you, love. This is your weapon. You will answer me.*

A smile began to spread across my face, of focusing bliss—

"Hey!"

Garcia. Garcia had hold of my ankle.

"Hey, Hawk. You catatonic on me? In ten minutes you got sunstroke?"

I smiled. "I'm fine, Ray."

"We need to head back in. Shoot. Want a beer?" He held up a can.

"No thanks . . . was it Mosley? What did he want?"

"Wanted to know where you were and what you thought of this boat. Wanted to know when we planned on doing some diving. Wanted to know if we'd been doing any diving." Garcia scowled. "Screwball. Screwball is what it is. Y'know, he's doubled guard shifts at all installations and is having Island Security string out more sensors, like we don't have enough already. You ain't seen it maybe but he's got everybody in The Area uptight. He's been picky as hell lately. Coleman's been gabbing a lot about ex-president Renwick, like he did during the campaign when he thought Renwick had CIA tailing him."

"Did Renwick have CIA tailing him?"

"Hawkins. I checked that back and forward." Garcia shook his head.

"Well? You're not answering my question."

"Look. You see how we've been operating. Mosley learns shit from CIA not even Randy Duncan hears."

"Do you really think so?"

"Hell yeah. Man, back channel is the only channel in intel."

"So Renwick didn't have CIA harassing Mosley."

"He may have thought he had but we nixed it. At least we're pretty sure."

"What do you mean by that, Ray?"

Garcia shrugged. "There's rumors of some weird shit part of CIA's been involved in."

"Weird shit."

"Yeah. Hokey stuff. Weird crap no one serious takes serious."

I hunkered down on the hull of the submarine. Ray's head poked up from the tiny hatch. "Tell me what you mean by that."

Ray laughed. "Look. You've seen Coleman up close. He's screwball. He claimed somebody was messing with his mind. Now don't fucking laugh. Somebody messing with his mind. Doing dangerous things. Putting ideas of suicide in his head."

"You're not kidding."

"I told you, Hawk. I hear a snicker and I'll throw this can of beer at you."

"I'm not snickering, Ray."

"Well I am. It's like the dumb shit you see on the tabloids at supermarket checkout counters. Palm readers and aliens. The inane shit women with rollers in their hair read and think is maybe real."

"You don't think that some of them know it's real."

"Shit. You'd make a good straight man, you know that? I knew you'd play this for a hoot. You've never hung out at a beauty shop next to a trailer park."

"How does this relate to Mosley, Ray?"

"The mind control stuff? Coleman blamed a lot of his erratic behavior during the presidential campaign on these thoughts. At least he had sense not to say it to the fucking press."

"Who'd he tell about these thoughts?"

"As far as I know, me, his wife, a preacher friend. Mosley doesn't trust shrinks and neurologists."

A slow swell rocked the submarine. There was a breeze, a fresh breeze from the east. The sub rose, dipped.

I waited until the swell passed and said: "That's good sense on Mosley's part. Shrinks are ill-informed about many things."

"Yeah . . . don't tell Mosley I said he was screwball. You won't, I know you won't. But you know what I mean though, don't you?"

"Yes, Ray. I know."

Evening and there was no moon. The stars were hard diamonds and as darkness fell the breeze from the east increased. I sipped a cup of hot mint tea on the patio of my secluded villa and watched the wind whip the bay, the starlight revealing the turbulent white combs of the waves. I could hear the wind pitch and twist the leaves of the palm trees.

The moment of dread was intense.

The sudden dread tightened about me, gripped me, slammed me.

Shuddering, I spilled the tea. I fought back. I managed to slap the teacup down on the patio ledge, the china shattering. I watched my hand continue to shake. I spun around. I saw myself mirrored in the glass facet of the patio door. I saw a frightened man in the reflection.

The reflection blanked, a connection broken.

I focused my capabilities, trying to reconnect, fearing the cause of the extrasensory dread.

The dread passed, as that afternoon the swell had passed, briefly tilting the vessel, until once again the submarine had steadied; dread passed like a wave of what the constricted language of physics calls gravity passes through the strange broken continuum that is the universe, fluctuating, minutely displacing energy and time, the ripples cutting gaps and channels, opening alternative space, until the ripples diminish and the universe resubstantiates.

Yes, the sick dread passed but it shook me hard. I thought of several things. I considered a possible physical basis—exhaustion, chemical imbalance, clandestine exposure to mind-altering or depression-inducing drugs. I rejected them. Something had gone terribly wrong. *Something is going terribly wrong. Was that a broken communication from Chatterley?*

I considered Prism. Damn you, Chatterley.

I went to the stove. It was a propane stove with a white porcelain surface. I turned on the burner and put the teapot on the eye.

By the time the water boiled I had rejected Prism. I had not decided what I would do.

The alert chime on the villa's security system rang. Someone was coming up the pathway to the front porch. I went to the video monitor. I punched the porch camera, selecting the light intensification lens.

The picture blossomed. It was Sari. Her face was turmoil. The wind blew her long black hair and pressed the sarong against her body. She walked unsteadily. She reached the porch, and there, for a moment, she began to fix her face, to reconstruct her dignity, to arrange the necklace, the sarong.

* * *

I met her at the door and brought her in. How quick, how professional her mask, the turmoil of her face erased by the cool arrangement of her eyes, the hauteur of her high cheekbones, the lithe appearance of a knee in the split of the sarong. There was an attempt at conversation. It was an embarrassing attempt. She fiddled with the necklace, a string of pearls that failed to hide the stitched rope of shaman scars around her neck. She started to say she had just been walking. Her eyes kept darting. She tried the pretense of accident, the I-happened-to-be-in-the-neighborhood lie.

The pretense cracked.

"I don't sound convincing, do I?" she said. "Damn wind."

"You sound better than you did a second ago. Here, sit down."

She didn't take the chair. A moment later, standing in the middle of the room beneath the overhead fan, she said, "Get me a drink, Carey."

"Sure . . . What's wrong?"

"I'm unsettled. I'm tired. Tired of *it*." She pounced on the word as though "it" signified utter Hell. She ran her hands up her long, elegant arms. "My head aches and I'm chilled." She glanced toward the wall, at the videophone, at the camera chip.

"The camera isn't on," I said.

"I don't care if it's on. They can take or fake all the pictures they want."

I gave her a shot of whiskey.

She took a sip. Without asking she sat on the end of the bed. I sat down next to her.

There was no dread, only desire. She put the shot glass down on the floor. She gave her mussed hair a toss. Our hands touched. My hand touched her throat. I kissed her full on the lips. Her arms enveloped me. There was no pause.

She lay next to me, looking at the wood beams of the roof. We listened to the wind. It would not die.

"Carey," she said.

"Yes."

She rolled over, against me, on top of me, her breasts crushing against my chest, her legs supple, muscled. Her lips covered mine. Her body was cool and firm and so agonizingly open. Blessed curse.

About 1:00 A.M. she sat up.

I knew but I rejected what I knew.

"What's the matter?"

"It's back, Carey."

"What's back?"

"The goddamn headache, Carey. Feels like a puncture wound in my brain."

"What do you mean."

"I mean on and off dammit. Cruel thoughts."

"Thoughts."

"Taunting thoughts." She shook her head, shook it hard. "Knives then bricks. Like greeting a razor blade and a wall, waiting for a wall of ice to crack."

I grasped her wrist. She felt like ice. "Blank then suddenly overwhelmed. That's the way it happens?"

"Yes," she hissed. "That's it. Have you had them too? Electronics? Is it something from the bugs?" She ripped her wrist from my hand and ran to the bathroom. She threw up. Moaning, she wiped her mouth on a towel. She cast a glance into the bathroom mirror. She froze. The reflection terrified her. *I saw it terrify.* She gagged, bent forward, and jammed the towel tight against her mouth, the terry cloth there, like a dam, as if the cotton could keep the choke down, keep the lies in check. She coughed into the towel.

With a dizzy step she left the bathroom. The moans stopped, stopped cold. She stared at me as if I were the stranger mirror. Then she threw the towel against the wall and she began to spill. She said she intended to help Said Farah Hassan escape. If she could find him. She said she intended to kill Mosley, if she could get to him. She said she was tired of it, it, the utter Hell. She was ready to go back to the Arab bastard she'd lived with before he sent her to Mosley, but that wasn't likely, was it? The emir had once said he loved her, but then Bandar had allowed her to go to work for Mosley, lent her like she was a tool, albeit a highly trained tool. The spill didn't stop. She didn't try to stop. Sari said many things, not giving a damn about electronic eavesdropping devices and monitors. She said she didn't care who knew and if Mosley had her killed, so what? Maybe she would spill to the press if there were anyone in the press Mosley didn't own.

Distracted, erratic passion, her escape—suddenly she slammed her fists against the side of her head. "That wall," she hissed.

I got very angry. Not at Sari. I directed my anger at Chatterley. Sari went back into the bathroom, her head a heap in her open palms.

"Give me the diamond ring you're wearing."

"What?" Her face crooked with pain and surprise.

"Please. Now, dammit!"

She shrugged, a crooked shrug, and took the ring off. "I feel sick again, Hawkins," she said. "So very fucking sick . . ."

I went into the kitchen. I stood by the stove, next to the refrigerator. I brought the flawless one-carat diamond up to the bridge of my nose, focusing the prism. I shut my eyes.

Stop vexing her, damn you! I am your weapon, use me!

The intense brilliance—

And for what can be measured as a fraction of a second or understood as a fold in eternity *I* was inside of *her* and I saw what she saw though there was no fulfillment, no completion, no tapping of her knowledge and the resonance—her shrill reaction, her rejection, Chatterley's *anger* at my intrusion, Chatterley's own terrible sense of isolation, her intense worry about the mission, the changing mission—shook me, shook my capabilities, shook my bones.

My eyes sprang open. I dropped the ring and fell to my knees. I knew I had succeeded in the transmission. The changing mission? I suspected I would be punished. I am a soldier, not a commander. I am a doer, not a seer. But I knew I had been correct in my assessment. Chatterley's intermittent jealousy—as my commander she put the operation at risk if her emotional components sapped her focus.

I went back into the bedroom.

Sari sat on the edge of the bed. I slipped the ring back on her finger. She was quiet now. She put the sarong on. "I'm going back to the emir," she mumbled. "Yes," she said. "That's what I will do."

She squeezed my hand as she left.

I watched her leave. Her walk was tired, not elegant. The gale wind had calmed to a breeze. I stood on the patio. The ocean was still disturbed and roiled. I was disturbed and unsettled. I felt a new tug of dread, like a slow tug of the tide.

The two shots of whiskey I downed didn't do much for me except make me want a third stiff pull. I rejected the third shot. I put on my bathing suit and grabbed a towel. The hell with it—I left my beeper on the bed.

I walked to the edge of the beach. The sand still felt warm on the soles of my feet. The breeze was flagging but the waves hit with a ragged ferocity. I started walking toward the grove near the palmetto swamp. I forced myself not to reflect on the events of the immediate past. The barriers I constructed were barriers I knew would work. I thought about Jessica. It was easy thinking about my wife, her bright smile, the fresh breeziness of her hair. It was not so easy thinking about Courtney. As I walked it became difficult, more burdensome with each step.

The lick of the surf reached my toes. Despite the

gale the night sea was warm. I threw the terry towel
back up onto the sand and dived into the breaking
wave, the surge refreshing.

I felt the tug of riptide. At least I thought it was the
tug of the riptide, a force of the physical sea. I stroked
with the current, not against it, the objective to get
ahead of the flow, to be faster than the current, so I
could maneuver, so I could exert some control over my
fate, my strokes and the current taking me out into the
bay then back along the beach, around the dark jut of
the sand spit beyond the palm grove, where I could
see the trees in dark silhouette, a dozen more strokes
and the slowing tide drifted into a calmer eddy where
the brine stream left the palmettos.

I was aware of the shark. The shark was not large, no
more than three feet long, but for a dog shark it had
the wolf attitude, the aggressive veer in its approach. I
startled. Then I realized the shark did not want me. I
shuddered when I saw what drew the shark into the
shallows. *I understood my dread.* The small shark,
disturbed by my presence, circled off.

As I touched the body, grasped it by the wet suit
and dragged it from the surf, I understood. A communication had failed, a broken communication at the
moment-of-death crisis when the able need no prism.

I dragged the body of Mick Fazzari into the palmetto jungle. I unstrapped the rebreather. His hand
had been mangled, as if by a blast. He had lost his fins.
The face plate of his diver's mask was cracked and the
pressure bruises on his temples, the crush of the right
side of his skull, suggested concussion, possibly by

either antidiver concussion grenades or an antidiver mine. I searched for anything. In the nylon-net equipment bag tied to his waist I found an extra diver's mask—one of *my* own masks—and a pair of fins. In his ops bag I found two underwater detonator cubes and several underwater "confusion" circuit boxes, of the type used to deceive marine sensor systems.

In his dive vest I found a quartz prism. I put it in the pocket of my swimsuit.

I didn't need Chatterley to tell me Mick had arranged an extraction. Common sense said that. I unstrapped the knife from my friend's leg. I dragged my friend's body into the swamp and slid it beneath the brine-soaked hulk of a palm log.

What in the hell is going on? I thought.

I hid the detonator cubes and circuit boxes beneath an exposed crop of dead coral. The knife, fins, and mask I took with me. I picked up my towel where I had left it on the beach.

My first plan was a plan hatched in terror. I considered the submarine. I would steal the minisubmarine. There were a half dozen islands within a hundred kilometers of Mosley's Island. With real luck and a lot of residual design I could reach one of the islands within seven hours. If I killed Garcia and took his body with me the presumption would be we were training. I could set a time charge, exit the sub near one of those islands, and, as I swam for the beach, let the sub plow on toward deep ocean, where the charge would explode and sink the little steel and titanium bastard.

Then I moved to aircraft. Filching a plane was possible. I would have to move fast. I wondered if I could burn out another human being's brain, one of the guards patrolling the flight line as an example. Chatterley has done it. But she is the exception, she is the foundation. My capabilities are those of an extension. But as someone with capabilities, rather than end up dead like Mick, could I, in a moment of life or death, kill silently by killing with my mind, telepathically strangling the life-directing circuits of the guard's brain? If only I had trained for such an operation, I thought, if The Shop had exercised my capacities, developed them, added them to my arsenal. But then I might be Chatterley, and I cannot be Chatterley. These mad thoughts, brief experiments, raced through my mind. I knew I could not be Chatterley. I am her soldier.

By the time I returned to my villa, morning nautical twilight had begun and I had gotten control of my fear. Sari—she had said so much. Could the electronics have missed her cries, her breakdown? I vaulted the fence and climbed up on the patio. From there I scanned the beach, the bay, looking for a mother ship, for an overturned commando boat. I saw nothing. I went into my villa, threw on my clothes, strapped my throwing knife to my leg, filled a canteen with water, and threw some fruit and candy bars into a rucksack with the mask and fins.

I picked the beeper up from the bed.

That was the moment I looked at the computer screen. The screen was blinking. "You have received urgent video E-mail," the computer voice said. "Please respond immediately."

The call light on the beeper was glowing.

I punched the reply button on the computer keypad. I tapped my code.

The Seal of Mosley appeared on the screen. The bald head of Mosley appeared on the screen. But the video mail did not continue. The image froze.

I tapped a quick reply. "Mail message did not arrive. 0400 hrs. Hawkins."

I logged off the computer. I picked up my rucksack and went to the door. I decided I would take the beeper with me as far as the swamp.

I saw the flashlights along the beach, the group of men creeping up the beach, the lights dropping, rising like hard white eyes. The helicopter came over the trees on the far side of the bay, the sound of its engine muffled by the distance and the sea breeze but its red running lights and swiveling searchlight giving it frightening definition. I started to run down the path to the road.

I heard the jeep driving up the road.

The jeep stopped beside me. He put the flashlight in my face. Garcia had been drinking. Ray tugged at his mustache. "Out for a stroll?"

"Thinking about a swim, actually."

In the harsh edge of the halogen beam Ray looked as macabre as he did angry. "Somethin' blew out a string of new sensors. Something using a dive sled. At least that's what the computer determined from the sound sensors that got a lock on the signal."

"Only dive sleds I know of are in the sub."

"And those are still in the sub. I checked . . . well, you gettin' in?"

"I said I was thinking about a swim."

Garcia's voice rose. "Dammit, Hawk. Get in. Orders from the Employer. We go back to The Area. Now. And he ain't asking pretty please."

"He isn't, huh."

Garcia put the flashlight down. From the pocket of his safari jacket he pulled a nine-millimeter automatic pistol. "Get in, whoever you are," he said. He pointed the pistol at my head.

That was the moment I concluded Chatterley had abandoned me and the mission, if there ever was a mission other than conspiring to compromise me. I was desperate, but no, I did not resort to Prism, I did not attempt any sort of physical escape or psychic connection. I did not attempt to burn Garcia's mind, however that might be accomplished by someone with greater abilities than mine. But I shielded myself and raised the barriers, strangely apprehensive . . .

They had me change clothes, dress in a gray jumpsuit. I palmed the crystal prism and dropped it into one of the jumpsuit's side pockets. They handcuffed me before takeoff. Garcia flew us to The Area in a 747 air freighter. I got into the lavatory once, to see, for a moment, in the narrow metal mirror above the wash basin, a pair of frozen brown eyes sinking into a set of darkening, middle-aged rings.

As the time passed I knew I would have to ensure my own survival and the survival of those innocents put at risk by my action. So I prepared myself. You know, the mind tricks itself, the mind constantly tricks itself. At times, in the interest of survival, the psyche must defend itself from the material world. Prisoners isolated in solitary cells will occupy their minds with mathematical equations, the reconstruction from memory of pointillist paintings. Individuals subjected to intense pain know that their minds can literally short-circuit the torment. This happens in dreams when the nightmare becomes too intense, too plausible. Belief and disbelief are simultaneously suspended. I knew from my own training and experience that for those of us with psychic sensory abilities, creating the illusion of distance from the material universe actually enhanced capacities. *I* would enhance my capacities. From that moment on I treated everything as if it were a terrible, compounding dream and I was nothing except a virtual sketch of myself in a sequence of beastly, evil neural outlines of events where no one was as he or she should be.

Damn you, Chatterley. Damn you.

Eleven

Back in The Area, Coleman Mosley got straight to the point.

"I admit I do not know precisely who you are, Hawkins . . . but I know enough." The crow's-feet bit around his ice-calm eyes as Mosley punched a button on his desk.

Courtney's face flashed on the giant wall video screen.

My insides cringed, guts gripped by a dozen nooses.

Courtney looked composed. She had the serenity of her mother, the composure and dignity I worshiped.

The close-up of Courtney clicked off. A new picture appeared: Courtney in a room with green wood-slat walls. She sat on a white flokati rug, reading a book. She wore a gray sweatshirt with a U.S. Air Force Academy logo. There were no windows in the room.

"Seems your daughter is very uncommunicative.

Practically a mute. Tough little gal. Won't even state her name. Though we know her first name is Courtney. . . . She seems as alien as you. You aren't planning on denying that this fine young lady is your daughter, are you?"

"I've never seen her before," I lied. Strange, if he didn't know her last name.

"Tut," Mosley replied. He slapped his desk with a bony hand. The model train engine sitting next to his pen set fell to its side. Mosley punched another button. A huge chart appeared on the video, three parallel charts. "DNA sequences," Mosley said. "The top one is yours. The one below it the sequence from a lock of hair found in a locket around the young woman's neck. The bottom sequence is the girl's. Ninety-nine percent chance of paternity."

I finished looking at the chart and turned to face Mosley.

"I know you are someone very dangerous. Perhaps you were meant to be dangerous to me," Mosley said. The glint in Mosley's eyes hardened. "You know there's a conspiracy to kill me."

I stared at him. "Tut," I replied. Curt, cold.

A slow crimson rage began to scorch in his face and neck. His brow wrinkled, his hands arched on the desk top. His lips quivered.

With a stroke of his long red handlebar mustache he doused the rage in favor of tranquil fury. "I'll kill you. I'll kill the girl. It's that simple."

"You'll withdraw that threat or you won't leave this room."

Mosley stared into my eyes. I knew he believed I could carry out my threat. Perhaps a part of my own mind, an assassin sector I am not trained to use or control, had entered his brain.

I was also certain that any movement I made was covered.

The red dot of a targeting laser appeared on my chest. The beam fell from the ceiling.

It was the precise moment to flinch. When you are the bull's-eye they expect you to squirm. Knowing full well I was under constant scan by cameras and electrodes, my thumb slipped down to the edge of my jumpsuit's side pocket. It brushed the prism I'd taken from Fazzari.

"I'm not stupid, Hawkins, or whatever your name is. There's a nine-millimeter barrel linked to the laser range finder," Mosley said. "It moves on a servo. The computer directing it has a digital image of its . . ." He paused a moment, then said with hard drama: "Target."

The computer responded to the voice command. On the video screen: weapon picture from the ceiling camera directing the laser targeter.

I looked at the video screen. I did not look like a frightened target.

"Doors," Mosley said.

Two doors on either side of the room slid open. Two bodyguards dressed in black leather, lithe, swarthy men I did not recognize, stood at the ready.

The picture of Courtney in the room with green slats returned to the huge screen. She leaned over her book. The brute red dot of a targeting laser appeared, dazzling in her fall of long auburn hair.

The targeting laser centered on my daughter's forehead.

"It would be simultaneous," Mosley whispered. "Both of you."

I thought several thoughts.

Damn you, Chatterley.

My thumb slipped away from the crystal and I felt utterly powerless. I felt abandoned.

I am falling into Hell—

Mosley waited. Then he nodded and said, "Doors shut."

The doors closed.

I closed my mind. I stared at Mosley.

"We know there was a diver out. Were you to meet him? Hawkins? You answer me."

"I was doing some diving."

"You were, huh. Well, dive this. We're looking for a body," Mosley grinned. Mosley punched another button. Courtney, now picking up a magazine, disappeared from the video screen.

A picture of a car wreck appeared.

Barb Angleton lay slumped against the wheel.

"There was no identification on this old gal," Mosley said, his twang vibrating with restrained irritation. "Obviously someone sold you out. My sources in Washington were notified about this here wreck."

"I don't follow that it's a sellout that I have a daughter and someone discovered her."

Mosley cocked his head. "I've thought that too. That's why you're still on the planet, cowboy . . . Now let's do some bidness. This wreck occurred last night. Just south of here."

At the moment of dread? I asked myself. The broken communication wasn't Fazzari's death, was it? Was it Courtney? Courtney could have capacities, the genes for ableness. *She could be a new Chatterley. Is that the problem, you bitch?*

"Like I tol' you, there was no ID on the ol' woman, nothing but a pack of Marlboros. The young lady was drugged."

"She was?"

"Yup. She was. Barbiturates."

Damn you, Chatterley.

"Who is this woman?" Mosley continued.

"I don't know," I replied.

"You know I've got about a hunnert sensors probing your body. Lessee what happens with your responses to my questions." Mosley punched a button.

Digitized charts measuring my heart rate, blood pressure, and a dozen other scans, measuring the physical attributes of life, appeared on the video screen.

I had no fear of a lie detector measuring physical attributes.

"Is the sky blue."

"Yes."

"Is your name Hawkins."

I let my abilities control my body. "Yes."

I am well trained. There was no change in any of the measurements.

"Who is this woman?" Barbara Angleton's face was superimposed on the digital graphs.

I said I didn't know and not one frequency fluctuated.

Mosley watched for the slightest deviation. Finally, he said, "You are perplexing . . . truth, lies, sun, moon—hell, I guess shit and Shinola are the same with you, huh?" His pupils shrank to hard black pins. "You're a hell of a weapon, Hawk. Not much of a family man but a hell of a weapon . . . I guess I'll have to kill your child."

My heart cringed. The monitor on my blood pressure spiked.

Mosley's tight grin formed beneath his mustache.

"So . . . little blood pumps occasionally, huh."

Mosley punched a button.

A new face appeared on the video screen.

"First target. Former president Renwick," Mosley breathed. He looked at me out of the corner of his eye. "Don't damn me in that mysterious mind of yours, Hawkins. And yes, I know it's mysterious. I've acquired some Russian equipment, the stuff the Sovs used to measure electrical emanations and penumbras associated with ESP? The synthetic telepathy idea? No tut this time. I know about the Rooski ESP research. And yeah, it scares me. Like you almost scare me. But paranoia has its utility in life, don't it, if you've got the cash to do something about it."

The little grin turned savage. "Governments are archaic on this post–Cold War Brave New Patootie of a planet. From now on out he who communicates, informs, and pays for things is the government. TV and me," Mosley cackled. "Quite a combo. What I say goes, Hawkins, what I say is the New World Order. That's it. And with men like you I'll make it stick in any niche I see fit to take a nick of." He leaned across the desk, a hint of sweat glassing his bald head. "Renwick. Now why Renwick, you might ask, if you didn't fuckin' *know*." He grinned a nonsense grin. "So I'll explain it. Let's say Global Security Division has a little contract from an interested Middle Eastern party. Think there's an interested party or two out there in the sand? Whattaya say, Hawk, you know how oil and blood can mix, mix like fire. Le's call it Operation Desert Payback. Almost as good as Operation Just Desserts, if the client hailed from Panama."

Mosley hawed at his own asinine joke.

"Second target," Mosley barked. The face of President Randall Duncan filled the entire wall. Then the face shrank. Mosley chuckled as the face shrank to the size of a postage stamp, a granular flyspeck on the digital wall. Mosley waited. Then he said: "I could get bored, fast, waitin' on you to participate in this conversation. Now why don't you pretend I'm a talk-show host and you're here to jabber. We can chew the cud about money, weather, diets, copulation, and a couple of assassinations."

I did not reply, at least I did not reply to him.

Mosley balled his fists. "Okay. You want to go back to the heartbeat shit, or mebbe your kid?"

Chatterley? Do I want to go back? Renwick and Duncan as projects. Duncan, Chatterley, he wants Duncan!

I shrugged. There was no indication of mental heat. "Who's the client on Duncan?" I asked.

"Me . . . I said *me*. You pay attention and we'll get this country back on track."

"I'm to kill Duncan as well as Renwick."

"I never said that, did I? How could you conclude that?" Mosley replied with no inflection. His eyebrows arched.

"I understand your subtle request for discretion."

Do I understand your indiscretions, Chatt? I licked at my lower lip. I said, once more to Mosley: "Now I want assurances after I take care of your concerns that my daughter will be released and cared for."

A gleam widened Mosley's face. "I swear to it, Hawk. On my *personal* word of honor."

"Show me my daughter and let her see me. Let us talk. Just a radio link."

Mosley blinked. He punched a button. The medical scans of my biorhythms appeared on the video screen. He looked at the screen, then he looked at me. "No," he finally said. "I think not."

"She's been traumatized. I want her to know I'm all right."

My biorhythms didn't move a notch.

Mosley twirled his mustache. "We can tell her that. And we'll make it credible." His twang turned the word "credible" into a long, sharp weapon.

"If I agree to kill Renwick, will you at least let me talk to her? Put her on the screen. I'll talk to her. She won't have to see me. Let me see her."

On that statement my blood pressure and heart rate increased.

"Whattaya mean? Stage it like a TV talk show and you're the call-in?" he cackled. "That's good, Hawkins. Stop pulling my leg."

"Damn you. I want to talk to her."

"You'd stick to a script so there's no funny stuff?"

"What do you mean."

"I mean a canned call. Hello, dearie, I love you. Daddy's well."

"Of course."

"You wanta see her that bad, huh?"

I swallowed. I made submission look good and bitter. I burned the impression of submission into a hole
in the air directed at his mind. "I would like that
opportunity, Mr. Mosley. Yes." *I pushed it, the hole,
toward him . . .*

A smile with bad edges wrinkled beneath Mosley's
handlebar mustache. He leaned back in his execu-
tive's chair and gazed at the ceiling. I leaned forward,
pushing it. Mosley's head turned sharply, fear an
instant arc in his eyes. His fingers, his paranoia: The
laser snapped back on. I expected that. Yet I swear I
felt it, hot, red, dead center on the flesh.

I froze. "My leg went to sleep," I said.

"You almost died," he replied. His voice was
weak. "Sit back up."

As I sat back up my fingers slipped into the side
pocket, touched the quartz prism, withdrew it.

Mosley continued to stare at me. I gripped the
prism in my palm.

Then he looked away once again, staring at the
ceiling. His face looked taut and drained. Finally, he
rolled a white eye toward me. In the shifting, uncertain balance of his wits, the indulgence of unrequited
hate replaced paranoia. "The hell. It's . . . it's this
way," he snapped. "Kill Renwick, Hawkins. Make
absolutely certain there is no connection to me.
Essential. That's essential. Nothin' ever said like that,
huh, you just know to do it 'cause you *know.* Right? If
you're caught the girl dies. If the kill's vicious enough
to please the client, and he's a hard reptilian kind of
client, I—" He paused.

I clutched the hot prism in my hand. I felt the
facets burn. My eyes closed. *I focus. The burning—*

Mosley continued: "I might be . . ." *The electrodes and monitors record the focal pulse as a localized burst of radiant energy, a momentary singularity and I enter and he is bending—* "Let's us s-s-say I'll rule nothing out," he stuttered. *He bends—*

Mosley paused, as if listening to himself. He blinked.

I hold the focus, an instant eternity.

Like a chalk-faced automaton Mosley said: "Yes, we'll say I'll rule out nothin' about you seein' your li'l girl . . ."

The instant elapsed.

I released my grip on the crystal.

His giddiness disappeared.

As I analyzed my experiment Mosley began to get control of himself, a slow, robotic control. He shook his head. An artery or vein, there on his temple now moving to his forehead, pulsed. The clutch of blood vessel seemed to glow beneath his skin, a curl of heat now the awkward shape of a spider. "Yes," he muttered. "We won't rule it out. Won't rule . . ." His eyelids narrowed, quizzically. He knew he was missing something, some time. Mosley blinked, searching out the source of emptiness, the source of the hole in his conscious scope . . .

He filled the emptiness with bluster. "Hell," he said, slamming a fist on the table, "I won't even rule out lettin' you live and work for me a little while longer. Howzat?"

The video wall erupted with a hundred TV-screen-sized images, each showing Mosley's charming, grinning face, the pulse of the spider artery on his forehead.

"Thank you, sir."

"You understand what all I've told you?"

"Yes, Mr. Mosley."

He blinked. "You understand I haven't ordered nothing."

"Yes."

"Whoever you are, Hawkins—maybe it matters, maybe it doesn't. What matters is taking care of business. You take care of Renwick and Duncan, Mosley Synoptics will take care of you."

Mosley nodded, to me, toward the laser, toward the doors. "Doors," Mosley said.

The doors slid open. The guards waited in the exits until I left the office. The guards followed me down the hall.

Twelve

I have worked with the Secret Service. U.S. Secret Service agents are the best trained security police in the world. Whether guarding the current president or a former president or an aging first lady in an Arizona nursing home, the guard never drops. Secret Service agents think highly of their own abilities. The agents are quietly confident. They maintain a sharp mental edge and they are certain they have no equals. Their information network is vast, subtle, responsive. The dossiers they maintain on potential assassins are thorough and constantly updated.

Mosley interrupted my planning. "Renwick the bastard tried to have me killed," Mosley kept saying. "Like Kennedy and Castro, turnabout's fair play, ain't it? And Renwick hassled my kids, my own daughter." Mosley scowled. Then he would blink and demand a progress report. In the blink, in the evading pool of his eye, I would see the image of Courtney, my daughter, the form of her face, as if I were taking a snapshot of the image in his mind.

Courtney's image blossoms and fades, replaced by the color red, a petaled Rorschach splotch morphing to a hot laser dot.

"So howzit going?" Mosley carped. "The Renwick Kill. Howzit going?" The Renwick Kill. The bravado of names with valiant resonance thrilled Mosley, but at least this operation's moniker was direct and to the point.

"Well?" Mosley demanded.

No assignment is ever simple, I replied, especially with an opposing force as competent as the Secret Service. Every kill is complicated, and viciousness is an additional, unnecessary complication.

"Make it vicious," Mosley said. "You have to make it vicious," Mosley insisted.

"Goddamn you," I said.

"And it had better goddamn be perfect, given your interests," Mosley finished.

My interests.

Yes. I knew I would use Prism if I had to. Hell, some form of Prism was inevitable, wasn't it? Damn you, Chatt.

Mosley's operational and tactical intelligence was perfect. The information stream on Renwick's movements was real-time.

"Impressed, aren't you, Hawkins?" Mosley sniped as I observed a sequence of satellite photos following the ex-president's recent trip to Aspen. "Knowing, Hawk. That's what's important. Knowing. These days to know is to control." He tapped his bald head with an index finger. "I know more than CIA, at least more of what counts," Mosley cackled. "You, for example. CIA don't know nothin' about you. But me, I sniffed you out. Drugs, electronics, you know I could probe you if I needed to know more."

"Then why don't you, Coleman."

The smile disappeared. "Because I know enough, don't I?" He arched a thick eyebrow. "You perform and I've no intention of crossing you."

He blinked. I saw her image.

I did not reply.

With a punch of a button Renwick's current and projected movements out to ten days from TIME NOW appeared on the wall video.

"So get cracking," Mosley said.

Yes, every assignment is complicated. But the Renwick assassination went without a hitch. Mosley's information was complete. My skills and abilities—my ability to compensate—are what they are. Former president Renwick's ineptitude is what it is.

VDX explosive would be vicious, VDX in a large-caliber cartridge. The explosive bullet and the tung-sten penetrator would decimate him. The concept had been explored by various special operations forces. In the Middle East the interest had centered on using a Special Applications Scope Rifle (SASR) to knock out ballistic missiles before the missiles were launched. In the Persian Gulf War a Green Beret sniper, positioned deep in enemy territory, would have fired a .50-caliber round packed with VDX improved plastic explosive or similar material at the Scud while the missile was moving on its transporter or being prepared for launch. Penetrate the missile's guidance mechanism, even chink a tail fin and the missile would destabilize in flight and disintegrate.

Mosley said, suggestively, the Middle Eastern client enjoyed the irony of the weapon, "hittin' Renwick with a weapon designed to thunk a Scud." Mosley's eyes were wide, like small optic radars, seeking an approving grin, a hint I shared his terrible sense of humor. I kept my eyes blank, my mind blank.

I did not select a Barrett L82 or any other large-caliber Western-manufactured sniper rifle. After some experimentation in the field, at Mosley's Arizona ranch abutting the Mexican border, I selected the Hungarian Gepard rifle. The Gepard uses a 12.7-millimeter heavy machine gun round of 108 millimeters in length. They are "dumb" rounds, that is, the usual rifle and machine gun round, not guided by computers or lasers or millimeter wave or infrared heat-seeking targeting devices. Devices with numbers, lights, and bytes are merely the newest means of assisting Cain in the latest slaying of Abel. Dumb rounds, like rocks, like bone, still kill. The rifle weighs about fifteen kilograms (thirty-two pounds), so it is quite heavy. It is a meter and a half in length (almost five feet), so the Gepard is a bit unwieldy. But the rifle has a carrying handle and a bipod folding under the long barrel, a fine pistol grip with button safety, and using APT B-32 ammo at a hundred meters I consistently put my shot groups into a space the size of a quarter. The Gepard kicked like a twelve-gauge shotgun firing slugs. The optics mount contained a laser range finder and a multipower telescopic sight. The range finder does not direct the bullets but does show the shooter rather precisely where the rounds are being aimed, as well as determining to within a half meter the range from shooter to target. Out to twelve hundred meters I felt comfortable with the Gepard's accuracy. Beyond twelve hundred the VDX explosive rounds began to drift and tumble.

The Renwick shot would be at fourteen hundred meters.

I had to compensate for the drift and tumble.

Four guards and Hey-Zeus Rodriguez accompanied me to the Arizona ranch. The ranch house had television monitors in every room. The stable and tack room had television monitors and computer terminals. There were no horses in the stables.

Hey-Zeus sat at the breakfast table eating bran and yogurt. I sat down next to him. We talked about the weather, the desert. Then I asked if I might look at his necklace. "You got a crystal fixation?" he smirked. "These are nothing special. They aren't diamonds." He handed me the necklace. I examined the stones, the silver chain, and handed it back.

"Where do you find stones like that?" I asked.

"All over. Getting them worked like that is easy too. You want one? Here. I picked this up in the creek." He handed me a chip of clear quartz the size of a dime.

With a grunt Hey-Zeus returned to his bowl of bran.

That morning I shattered the crystal with a hammer. I kept the purest microfragment.

We needed an Arab with a past, and the client supplied one. His name was given as Abdul Aflaq. He had connections with the Abu Nidal terror gang, connections confirmed within the Interpol computer downlink Mosley maintained in The Area.

Mosley began to let CIA and the Secret Service "know" about Aflaq eight days prior to the kill. Aflaq made an appearance in Berlin, at a Turkish rally protesting neo-Nazi activities in the reborn, united Germany. Aflaq denounced the conspiracy of the West, the conspiracy to rob, strangle, and destroy the Islamic world. He specifically named Renwick as "the guilty."

Aflaq's speech ringed the world, courtesy of Mosley and CNN. CIA and the Secret Service responded. All of the various intelligence and police agencies immediately opened active files on Aflaq. Aflaq was a cause of concern. My deceit became a participatory fiction, with all agencies assuming its truth. And once the files are open—once the words are on the page or on the computer screen—disbelief becomes more difficult. The lie begins to live and breathe. Political and police careers become committed to its gospel.

Once the agencies had bit on the Aflaq ploy I flew to Berlin in the Citation.

Aflaq did not observe the Prophet's strictures against alcohol. And this evening the woman Aflaq's boss (Mosley's client) had "loaned" him "out of friendship" got our angry Abdul very drunk. Aflaq stumbled down the alleyway, stinking of licorice schnapps. He was mumbling to himself in Arabic, something about torches. He did not see me. I stood behind the trash cans. I fired the injector dart into his fat neck. He spun, the whirl of gravity and sedative (two cc's in the injector dart, with one hundred milligrams per cc of secobarbital) buckling his legs. His body flopped and slammed onto the soot-caked asphalt behind the dirty brown workers' apartment building in the former East Berlin, now just the ugly eastern half of Greater Berlin.

Two days later Aflaq appeared in Miami. A television microcamera monitoring the rear entrance to a gun store owned by a member of the anti-Castro Alpha 66 resistance group caught the briefest quarter-faced glimpse of a man resembling Aflaq. The beer bottle the man dropped in the barrel in the alley had a half dozen solid fingerprints that looked like those of Aflaq. The wiretap the FBI maintained on the phone line (a legal wiretap to keep track of the anti-Castroites' potential terrorist activities) recorded the short conversation. Aflaq's Arab accent interested the intelligence services. The CIA/NSA computer (with Chatt's help?) matched the recorded voiceprint with a voiceprint made of Aflaq's rant on CNN. Aflaq (or at least his voice) asked the gun-store clerk if he knew where one might buy four or five Soviet-type 12.7-millimeter heavy machine gun bullets, or at least their casings. He wanted to turn them into "novelty gifts" for a friend, specifically, cigarette lighters.

Four days later, in a moment of dreamlike objectivity, I left the drugged but unbound Aflaq in an efficiency apartment off of a Houston highway called Old Spanish Trail. The highway is a litter of gas stations, grocery stores, Laundromats, and strip joints now called gentlemen's clubs. At three in the morning the Trail's neon markers remained bright and awake.

The clouds were gray and low, the humidity high. Yes, I would have to compensate.

I drove the van into a town called Waverley, fifty miles north of Houston, a spot on the map not far from the interstate yet tucked into the loblolly pines and thickets. Waverley isn't far from a huge housing and business complex owned by Mosley. They play an international tennis tournament and a couple of golf tournaments there. The megadevelopment is named Woodforest.

As I stopped the van I thought of contacting Chatterley. I did not. I rejected the option.

I checked all of the information inputs. Renwick was having breakfast in the clubhouse. His golf clubs were on his cart. Looked good—I left the van, making my way on foot to the stashed rifle. As I entered the preserve north of Woodforest I punched a button on my belt. All sensors covering the approach to the nature preserve momentarily blanked. When the sensors snapped back on the security personnel would find that everything appeared to be in working order. Except a computer virus had invaded the interface between the sensors and their controlling computers. The virus told the central computer that all was normal when in fact I had entered a restricted area. When I left the virus would tell the seismic sensors that a human being of approximately Aflaq's weight had left via a path to the west. The virus would then erase itself.

From the hillock in the preserve, where the Gepard sat beneath a camouflaged tarp, I would have to shoot down the length of an almost 600-yard firecut in the woods, the length of the 424-yard seventeenth hole, the length of the 388-yard twelfth hole, over a small lake, and to the green of the third hole where in eight minutes

Renwick would be putting. All told the shot would be some 1,550 yards, or slightly over 1,400 meters.

Beneath the tarp I went through my operational checks on the Gepard and on the laser range finder.

I checked my mobile intelligence computer. The Secret Service helicopter was about to make its sweep of the golf course. It took off from near the clubhouse. Two minutes later it swung over the wood line, the racket of its blades and engine frightening the birds in the trees. It did not linger over the firecut. The helicopter was flown for both reconnaissance purposes and intimidation purposes. I was prepared to deal with the helicopter.

My computer reported that Renwick's tee time had been delayed.

I pulled out my compensator. I had punched a hole in a clear piece of plastic and inserted the small crystal microfragment into the hole. The square of clear plastic was set into a flip slide. I placed the flip slide at the end of the telescopic site and flipped it down over the lens. I looked through the lens. The tiny prism aligned dead center in the crosshairs.

Fifteen minutes later Renwick appeared on the third tee. I pulled off the camouflage tarp and checked the optics.

A Secret Service agent in a golf cart was inspecting the green. He looked around carefully.

My intelligence computer told me that the helicopter had landed. Good. Secret Service was trying to operate within its reduced budget.

Six minutes later Renwick reached the green. He was, as usual, playing by himself.

The Secret Service agents fanned out around the green.

I saw the short, hefty Renwick lean over his club.
He was in a sand trap. He made a crisp downswing.
Ball and sand flew onto the green, the ball coming to
rest perhaps thirty feet from the cup. A Secret
Service agent pulled the flag. Renwick kicked his
cowboy hat back on his head and eyed his tricky
putt. As he did so I placed the laser light beam on his
chest.

Renwick stood very straight (the target point now
his belly), then he leaned over the putt, the coherent
ruby light placing the flickering upper arc of its circle
on his chin.

The range finder bleeped. The light return had
diminished.

I don't need a laser range finder, not with the ability to compensate.

*Damn you, Chatterley. Let this ripple in your
mind and tear holes in your shrunken soul.*

I peered through the telescopic site into the facets,
into the erupting, blinding, focusing universe of the
prism. The rifle lurched. The bullet was now the
smartest of weapons.

The FBI and the Secret Service found Aflaq in the
apartment. Aflaq denied all knowledge of the assassination of Renwick. In the twenty minutes the FBI held
him he claimed he had no idea of how he came to the
United States. Aflaq appeared dazed and shocked,
according to information Mosley obtained from his
sources. "He's one vacant Arab," Mosley snickered.
Aflaq could not explain the 12.7-millimeter shell
found on the floor in the apartment, a cartridge with

his fingerprints all over it, a cartridge with the smell of cordite and trace plastic sheen of VDX.

American fighter-bombers struck Baghdad the next morning. "If we don't make 'em eat a few air strikes," President Duncan mused before the White House press corps, "we're jellyfish." Seven days of closely coordinated air and missile raids followed, seven days of de-creation and reverse Genesis in Mesopotamia. This time, I noted, the bomber jocks struck the oil fields in Mosul and Kirkuk, the wellheads melting in geysers of black and orange flame. Land-attack cruise missiles smoked the petrochemical production facilities along the Tigris and Euphrates Rivers, the burnt refineries and catalytic crackers televised by CNN looking like charred locust husks and withered Erector sets.

Within three days, I noted, Rotterdam spot oil prices rose eight dollars a barrel, West Texas Sweet rising by almost nine.

The sour taste ringing my mouth surprised me. The sour didn't disappear, despite antiseptic mouthwash and a gallon of hot mint tea. So I asked Mosley, with discretion, why the client would want to bring destruction on his own land.

"Whoa. You don't understand much about the politics of perception or the Middle East, do you, Hawk?" Mosley replied without sarcasm. Then he added, his bald head wrinkling and his eyes narrowing to parallax: "Now, I never said the client lived in Iraq, did I? Well? Good gosh, the oil business is global, ain't it? I never said who or what or squat about anyone being from Iraq, no sir. By damn I didn't."

Thirteen

C ourtney," I said.

"First things first and second things second," Mosley said. "Now fer the Duncan Kill."

"Duncan."

"The president," he said.

I couldn't figure the presidential kill.

Chatterley—killing Duncan cannot make sense, even to you.

I lost control. I exploded. "Coleman. This horror is going too far."

"What choice you got, Hawk?" Mosley interrupted.

Choice. I see the face of Chatterley. Since firing the bullet at Renwick, since guiding the weapon, the trace of her lovely face, like the suggestion of a waxing moon, has hung suspended in the mental space—

"Any probs with that, Hawk?" Mosley asked. His face and head wrinkled, the mustache rising, drooping.

"You agreed to show me my daughter."

"Did I . . ."

I gritted my teeth. "You did. I want to see for myself that she's okay."

"And you're not a man to cross, eh Hawk?" Mosley smirked. "Okay. But you know the rules. You see her but she doesn't see you. And she can't talk about anything except hello, how are you. You be damn sure she follows the rules."

The close-up clicked on. Once more Courtney was in the room with green wood-slat walls. She sat on the same white flokati rug, looking distraught. The gray U.S. Air Force Academy sweatshirt looked as if it hadn't been washed in two rumpled weeks.

"Daddy?" she asked nervously. She wrung her hands. "I'm thinking about Mommy. Oh Daddy, can you see me?" Her left hand gripped her right hand in a mime of intense nervousness.

Good, I thought. *Good girl.* I focused on her image on the wall screen.

"First damn words she's muttered since we nabbed her," Mosley said. I knew he was staring at me. I ignored him.

"I see you, dear," I said. "Are you all right."

"Yes," she said. "Sort of. Sort of sad and lonely."

But her hands did not say yes. Her hands signed: "No. Flu."

I said: "Don't try anything foolish, Courtney. You know you cannot say anything about where you are. Please don't try to."

"I won't," Courtney replied.

But her hands, in the scrambled sign language, the

subtle code of her dead, deaf mother, spelled out: "Tetons, lake, Dodos, sensors," and I knew, and there was little mystery. Dodos—she had had a pet Doberman named Dodo. It became the word for vicious dogs she had learned to control.

"Daddy. I'm scared. I thought I was old enough to be safe. But I'm scared."

"You'll be all right, Courtney. No one's old enough to be safe. Don't lose your head and don't be a dodo."

She suppressed the flash of a grin. "I've told them nothing," she said in a stern, adolescent voice. Her hands said: "Three guards near."

"Things will be all right. You're doing fine."

"I want to believe you, Daddy."

I felt a radiance in my mind.

"Trust me, dear."

"I trust, therefore I worry," she said with intensity as her hands spelled out "Wyoming maybe?"

"You're plucky, Court. Stay plucky."

"Yes, Daddy." She smiled. "You be sensible. You can be sensible."

"I'll try. Good-bye, dear."

"Good-bye, Daddy."

Her image faded from the wall screen.

"Damn," Mosley said. He was amazed. "What a nice sweet voice. And I'd have sworn she was a mute." His gaze hardened.

Discipline. The word in Mosley's brain. I saw the word in Mosley's brain. I felt the idea in his mind like an object with tactile reality. *The son of a bitch is frightened by Courtney's discipline.* Then I scared— had I placed the word there?

I didn't say anything. I know I blanched. Perhaps I shook with a disgusting, appealing nausea. A perfect probe, almost elicitation—or a placement? I really goddamned was increasingly able. *Able in Mosley*—

Yes, I had experimented, on three or four occasions I had placed thoughts, fired my thoughts like bullets into another mind. Yes, I had placed but it was really useless placement, placement with no desired effects. My experiments were gentle, they were gentle bullets, an idea placed in Jessica's mind, in Courtney's, in their able uncloaked minds. They encouraged my experiments. And Courtney experimented. Courtney's ability—it's scary. I knew she'd be damned with the gift. Jessica—she did not need sound senses, she was able in embryonic but unusual ways. The Shop brought us together for procreation. The Shop brings ables together since genetic engineering can't crack the DNA code. Despite The Shop forcing us on each other, I fell in love with Jessica. Jessica had abilities as well as my adoration. No wonder Chatterley hated her. Before Jessica died I promised her, about Courtney. After Jessica's death I told The Shop to leave my child out of it. Keep Jessica's child out of your goddamned designs. *Yes, that's still the deal*—

Of course the original tests The Shop ran on me showed I had the rudimentary ability to place. To a certain degree my ability to place is why I was made into a weapon. Guiding the bullet telekinetically, my mental guidance focused through a crystal, must be—once the science is understood—must be a peculiar form of placement, an act in this vicious universe imitating the placement of idea from mind to mind in

mental creative space. And in that universe ideas are
weapons. Newspapers, talk shows, Hitlers are predi-
cated on this insight. The explosive, destructive sound
bite dominates politics—it always has and will, from
the angry demand for skulls by the tribal chieftain to
the coolly televised analysis of essential national interest by the commander in chief.

The wannabe commander—I examined Mosley's
hardened gaze. Yes, I'd placed, placed words in the
crudest of ways, knowing my abilities were limited,
but experimenting, always wondering if placed words
might lead to directing ideas. *Discipline.* But I had
never been able to elicit. Eliciting is an escalation, a
step beyond mere placement. Chatterley places and
elicits with ease. She elicits thoughts, entire memories. When the energy is there, when the focus is perfect, she can elicit entire memories—tactile, real—as
concrete and present as the word "discipline" I had
encountered in Mosley's mind.

Entering the enemy's mind is the act of the ultimate intelligence operative. Forget the high-tech jargon, let the psychologists eat screws. Power hunger,
the drive for weapons, spurred the research into the
mind's other capacities. Defense, personal defense,
drove my own experiments. I had placed the outlines
of thoughts but I had not been able to elicit and certainly not to direct. Chatterley—she had been experimenting with direction. The ultimate weapon: to have
control of your own enemy's will, to be, in effect,
your own enemy, have your enemy at your beck and
call when you need him, when you need headlines, a
cause célèbre.

Chatterley argued that Sun Tzu, von Clausewitz,

Caesar, Machiavelli, any thinker would have understood the concept, the warrior in them would have
seized the weapon, and the politician above them
would have used it. *To Direct*. To dictate to your
opponent. The Soviets explored it. Chatterley and
The Shop—how far had they gone? The search for
doubles, those who can direct another or act as a
focal lens for an individual with Chatterley's capabilities, that search for this ability produced few men or
women with useful assets. At least Chatterley told me
so. But here, this instance—I had entered Mosley's
mind. And I realized, inside the bastard's warped and
mean mental space, along its petty Napoleonic boulevards, in its stinking paranoid alleys, he and I were
not alone. There was another presence, a weak presence, a presence in position, by damn a lurking double preparing to act. . . .

The Renwick assassination jolted the Secret Service.
As the nation entered mourning, as if in an act of professional contrition the security personnel blanketed
President Duncan. From the Secret Service's point of
view an ex-prez is one thing, protecting the is-prez is
another.

But as planning for the Duncan Kill evolved I saw
the ugly interior of America (the interior control
structure, of which The Shop, the office of *Special
Highly-sensitive OPerations*, is its tentacle and I its
most poisonous sting) move its horrid monster body
and prepare to murder the semblance of democratic
will, to kill its own president, or at least to offer me
the opportunity (me, the damned) to slaughter him

on Its behalf. And the additional reasons for kidnapping Said Farah Hassan now became clear. Since I am merely a soldier, I am slow to put the details together into a whole, to fit the pieces. But Hassan fit.

"Fer sure," Mosley said, when I made the remark that at the moment in time selected, in the place selected for Duncan's murder, security would be unusually slack. "Fer sure, Hawkins. We got folks willing to let some things slide our way. People want to get this country moving again."

I tried to elicit, to enter again. I failed. No, it must have been a moment of unusual clarity, of energy I could not maintain.

"You ready?" Mosley asked.

I tensed.

I lay on my belly, flat on the dirt, beneath the canopy of oak and pine and Virginia thicket. I felt too ready. The acoustic, seismic, and light sensors had been easy enough to mislead, again using electronics and well-placed viruses, but the aerial watchdogs were another problem. The helicopter and the light UAV (unmanned aerial vehicle) reconnaissance drone swept the wood line. Forget the leaves, the trees, the brush, the vines, the rose and thorns. In the eye of heat-detecting and angled-radar sensors such obstructions do not exist. The green earth is useless clutter that can be erased. But I was prepared to blind them. The camouflage parka I wore not only changed my physical appearance but it absorbed my heat signature, the 98.6-degree glow of my body. Wrapped inside the heat-absorbing cloak, on the infrared camera in the drone I would appear as an unremarkable smudge in the cool magnitude of the forest, a flickering low-grade stain on the sensor clearly not a deer, not a rabbit, certainly not a heat source that was anything identifiably human.

Hello . . .

My head jerked up, my chin bumping the butt of the laser designator and targeting device.

The word faded, leaving only an impression.

I knew I had been probed, an idea placed. But not by Chatterley. The probe did not have the energy and power of Chatterley. Where were Chatt's loyalties, other than with The Shop and with herself? Surely The Shop had to know of Mosley's plan. Inside Mosley's mind I knew we were not alone—

A branch behind me cracked. I rolled, popping the silenced MP5 submachine gun up on my knee, my head breaking the tuck of the camouflage cloak. I waited. I focused. I felt the sweat on my forehead, the honing concentration of my senses, of all of my abilities. Not enough. I got nothing. Slowly, I brought the heat magnifier on my wrist to my eyes. There, in the infrared, I saw the mottled heat form. I lowered the heat sensor. A moment later the buck, its black nose breaking the brush leaves, stepped off the deer path. With a lithe flick of its head—smelling—it entered the thicket. Two does followed, last of all a yearling.

I crawled forward up the creek bed, through the clutch of vines and roots, ivies and honeysuckles.

I heard another aircraft engine sound.

A miniature Piper Cub passed overhead. No, not the UAV—it was a radio-controlled model airplane.

The Piper Cub climbed and banked.

A moment later the much larger reconnaissance drone reappeared. The unmanned drone passed over once more, perhaps a hundred meters east of me, at an altitude of fifty meters. The UAV banked, circling the horse paddock, turning toward Mount Weather.

The Mount Weather Complex in the far western corner of Virginia was designed as a near-to-Washington citadel for the president and Congress, an underground command site to protect America's highest political echelons and nabobs from the blast, shock, and radioactive fire of the thermonuclear holocaust, that deadly burning light two generations were certain waited at the end of the long icy tunnel called the Cold War. Originally the old building on the top of the hill, still outside the guard gate of the restricted site, served as an office for the old U.S. Weather Bureau. Mount Weather was a launch site for the first weather balloons. You get there by driving down the Beltway into Virginia, then heading west toward Winchester. At a rather innocuous-looking junction between the main highway and a county road you head south into a spur of the Appalachians.

The CIA used The Horse Farm at Mount Weather as a training and special operations development site. Mount Weather, however, served another governmental purpose. The Horse Farm sits above the five miles of tunnels where Congress and the Pentagon and all the other rats would burrow as the world they failed was being destroyed. The Horse Farm operated out of a series of single-story metal-frames, not far from a midnineteenth-century brick-and-stone stable. Over a period of years the stable was renovated. Horses appeared, at first nags, then thoroughbreds. Why shouldn't America's best racing stock survive the thermonuclear disaster? Besides, horses loping over the long grass avenues above the tunnels added to the cover story. The posh saunas and underground swimming pool came later. Aging senators safely encased in forty meters of concrete, steel, and lead, even as the surface world dies from nuclear poisoning, need not miss their squash games and massage therapy.

Of course, with the end of the Cold War, with the end of the Cold War being a whimper, not a bang, the Mount Weather nuclear survival complex appeared to be an anachronism. Enter President Duncan. Camp David wasn't his style, at least it wasn't when he was romancing the vice president's redheaded wife, Frances Masterson, the ex–rock star, the siren of several cutting-edge MTV rock videos. Frances Masterson loved horses, more than she loved her husband, more than she cared for President Duncan. She loved the fresh breeze on the wide meadow camouflaging the antique bunker complex. So the thoroughbreds remained stabled at The Horse Farm, oblivious to the end of the Cold War, well fed and curried.

Frances Masterson.

Is this why, Chatterley? I thought. I am a soldier. At times I am slow to grasp the larger issues, the evil human twists which shape us.

I clambered over an elbow of brush.

Hello . . .

I stopped. Yes, there was the thought again, an echo of a contact from someone able. Someone not Chatterley.

I touched the prism in my jacket pocket. I blocked. *Leave me alone,* I thought.

And there was no other voice in my mind.

At the edge of the field I peered across the beveled edge of the binoculars' alignment knob, squinting at the distant horse and rider. I brought the binoculars up the moment the horse and rider jumped the far fence.

Frances Masterson jumped with the cool pomp of English gentry, yet hit an open gallop with the controlled recklessness of a desert Arab.

Then she shifted in the saddle and waved to President Duncan, as he and five Secret Service agents stood at the tree line. And between two agents stood the first son, Hardin Duncan. He was manipulating a radio-control box. Was the boy flying the Piper Cub, playing catch with the recon drone? Clever of Duncan, nothing like taking your child along to mask an extramarital affair. *But if the boy isn't out of the way this mission is a scrub. I won't kill that boy. . . .*

The Piper Cub reappeared above the line of oaks. The toy airplane rose, stalled, then suddenly dived toward the horse and rider.

The horse suddenly cut, jumped, and reared. Mrs. Masterson lost her balance.

She hung on. Two Secret Service agents raced toward the horse and rider. The Piper Cub pulled up from its dive and headed across the field, in my direction. Mrs. Masterson and the horse bolted the other way. With the airplane gone the fox in this one-horse chase was invisible—frantic fear directed the animal. The roan stallion Frances Masterson rode along the distant split-rail fence seemed to set his own rash pace over a twisting, unpredictable course. I increased magnification. Mrs. Masterson, her red hair back in a bun, flexed forward in the black saddle, a riding crop flopping in her hand. Tan jodhpurs gripped the lean angle of her thigh. Her mouth tensed.

The tall stallion suddenly hooked away from the wood rails, bolting for the middle of the green Virginia field, then, turf cuts flying, swerved back toward the distant fence. The horse jerked to the right, out of the binocular lens, into the tree line of yellowing oak and ash. Then I caught the horse and rider once more, as the red-brown rump of the horse bobbed up and disappeared, the sudden jump clearing the fence, the horse and rider vanishing into a crack in the thick woods.

I scanned the wood line beyond the far fence—no horse and rider in the foliage breaks.

The helicopter and UAV both went after the rider.

Hardin Duncan's model plane had disappeared. And so had the boy.

The horse and rider reappeared. She now had the horse under control. Still nervous, the big black stallion panted and pawed. She dismounted. A Secret Service agent took the horse by the reins. Frances Masterson walked into the middle of the field, shaking her lovely head.

As President Duncan jogged toward her I flipped

on the laser range finder. The shot would be a kilometer.

My laser optics blanked. I punched the reboot. The laser was fuzzing—another laser was bathing Frances Masterson. *From where?* I followed the light wave to the source. Someone with a designator lay in the underbrush at the edge of the open meadow, a kilometer from President Duncan.

And the UAV, its motor suddenly revved, was flying directly toward the laser light.

The helicopter, loitering over the Mount Weather house, made a ninety-degree turn.

The Secret Service agents around Duncan suddenly jumped. Frances Masterson leaped back on her horse.

I froze. This was not the plan.

I shuttered the laser.

The radio receiver in my headband snapped on. "Round on the way," a voice chattered in nervy, very dialectic East African Arabic.

I flipped the power switch and with a silent whine the laser target designator lit.

Okay. Perhaps this was the plan. The larger plan, of callous, calculated betrayal on the grand scale, now on the small, intimate scale of my volition. In the large plan I am a soldier, a murderous pawn who moves with . . . with a predictable awareness. *A biological robot, Chatterley, that is what you have made me. And I am here to commit this horror. Were it not for Mosley's hostage I would rebel.*

But perhaps not. The momentum of the mission gripped me. I placed the hard cone of light on the running President Duncan and Frances Masterson, as she glanced over her shoulder at the UAV, as she brought her still-shaken horse into a canter beside him.

The plan: The Somalis Mosley had recruited from those we captured (and yes, Sari I am sure aided in the recruitment) had acquired a small truck. The modifications were simple. The three-quarter-ton pickup had what looked like an open bed. A quick inspection would show nothing. Two men driving in an empty pickup, four kilometers from the target point. They had the routine practiced, executable in seconds. The Global Positioning Satellite receiver (GPS) on the truck put them within two meters of their firing point when they stopped. In ten seconds the false floor in the pickup bed opened. The eighty-one-millimeter mortar appeared. The GPS was attached to a computer controlling the mortar that would fire the smart, precision munition.

Smart, precision munition. Surgical strike. These fool words, words like "precision" and "surgical." Only stupid mechanics and the nuts in Congress who finance them think death is precise, that the inherent fractal chaos of an explosion has anything in common with a surgeon's scalpel, that the slaying of human beings is in any way analogous to a surgeon's meticulous removal of a cancer.

But the vengeful Somalis were well drilled. In their own way they were most precise, human beings as precision weapons. The Somalis unlatched the mortar tube. The pneumatic piston raised the mortar from its plate hidden in the well of the truck bed. The computer

attached to the GPS achieved a firing solution in two
seconds, moving the piston, spinning the plate, correct-
ing the tube for angle of elevation. One Somali pulled
the mortar round out of the carry tray beside the mortar tube. The mortar shell his long fingers grasped and
placed over the mouth of the tube was a modified
British eighty-one-millimeter Merlin "smart round"—
greatly modified. The Merlin fascinates the mechanics
and the technical encyclopedists. The British smart
shell operates on millimeter wave. Using millimeter
waves the round "sees" the reflected angles of large
objects, trucks and tanks for example, and in the final
split seconds of attack guides itself to its target and to its
own destruction. The standard British Merlin shell has
an antiarmor warhead. The four shells Mosley had fab-
ricated, however, had laser targeting sensors in place of
the millimeter wave. The antitank warhead of the
Merlin had been replaced with a complex antipersonnel
warhead: high explosive, fragmentation splinters, and
steel fléchettes. The laser targeting sensor in the nose
of the elongated mortar round would detect and follow
my designator's beam—or the beam of the designator,
the unknown designator across the meadow, to the
presidential target. Unless the designator were blinded,
or eliminated, the mortar round would land within a
half meter of the running Duncan, the woman, the
horse.

And the Somalis on the truck succeeded. They
stopped. The mortar tube deployed in the truck bed.
The gunners checked the computer and confirmed
the firing solution. The firing sequence began. One
Somali made the short, encrypted broadcast over the
radio, which I heard. They dropped one shell. A

moment later—I am certain they did it on orders—the mortar men dropped a second. In the space of fifty seconds they had stopped, fired, and were moving again. That first high, arcing shell they fired was in flight eighteen seconds. The Somalis put the Dodge pickup into first gear at the moment that first shell—despite the kamikaze crash of the UAV and the explosion atop the Somali stooge with the laser designator, the man in the brush—that first shell splashed on President Duncan exactly where I placed the lasing ruby light.

Yes, the Unmanned Aerial Vehicle the Secret Service had up and circling had a laser sensor, for detecting laser designators and homing in on the source. In the most sensible of high-tech protective solutions, the UAV had its own seek and destroy capability—it was a mechanical robot, able to detect and act. The Secret Service goes to great lengths to protect the President.

The hefty dark-headed fellow with the jolly face and the thin, retired Air Force general who does the military analysis for CNN said the UAV counter-weapon system worked as it should. Yes, the UAV dived straight at the Somali. Indeed, the airborne robot's antipersonnel grenades blew the Somali assassin into tiny bits, just like the tests at Eglin said they would. That the mortar round that killed President Duncan did not go haywire, that it landed six feet in front of him, blew him to pieces, killed the horse, maimed the vice president's wife (her left leg required amputation), and wounded two Secret Service agents, well, that was just damned bad luck. Damned evil luck. And look what it produced. An American tragedy leading to an international nightmare of terrifying specifics.

The UAV blew up. I knew whatever Somali chump Mosley had weaseled into the Mount Weather compound, the man beneath the UAV, would be blamed. So I held the laser light on Duncan. The designator sensed the round which sensed the light. Above Duncan, Mrs. Masterson, the stallion, the entourage of Secret Service, the computer chip inside the smart mortar shell solved the equations and mapped the closing angles, its fins redirecting its flight path, the armed warhead's fuse detonating in front of Duncan and two feet above the thick green carpet of meadow grass. He evaporated in the orange and white blast.

I pulled back. One target, one round, one kill. The Somalis had dropped a second round. Well, let the second round hit where it would. I had to clear out myself now. I had to make it to the culvert five hundred meters through the forest. I had to get out of this for Courtney's sake. *Damn you, Chatterley*. I began to run, to sprint through the forest and bramble. The culvert connected to a drainage line sucking runoff from the field above the tunnel system. I would enter the drainage line, follow it a kilometer underground, then emerge in a creek bed. There I would pick up a trail bike which I would take up into the mountains to Skyline Drive.

With the camouflage cloak about me I scrambled backward, rolled into the ditch, then came up in a crouch, running down the thicket-filled ditch. Yes, let the second round hit where it would. And I heard the second mortar round, the first distant hiss—on the ground you start to tremble—then the whistle of its fins, its fins like razor nails clawing air. I heard the mortar shell begin to scream as it dived, a plummeting sphere of cold electronics and iron enlarging, magnifying, as I visualized—*saw the trap in my mind, the trap*—the radar energy of this shell's emitter, its homing sensor, a robot hawk locking to its destined, ignorant target. The shell plunged. I am certain I dropped the laser targeter in fear, as I threw myself down toward the thorn ditch, into the earth, the heat shriek of the shell driving vibrant into my ears.

I slammed prone into the ditch the same second the ground shook like muddy rubber and the world splintered. My hands gripped nothing, gripped my face, my head and arms grappled with the thorn roots, the twist of my body. Time and gravity spun in the substance of pain, the instant rake of the shrapnel, the crushing press to the bone. My mouth flew open and a gag of hot mud severed my scream. I coughed. The retch threw me forward. I was up, rocking on my knees, staring at the blue sky, sky at the end of the tunnel, a recessing blue drop of sky in a fusing cone of black, drowsing, spinning, shrouding blue outpost in darkness.

Nausea, blood, chucked out the nose. I pitched forward. My eyes closed, they opened. A moment passed, seconds, years of nausea. My mind, my ability—I lost consciousness for seconds. There was the cone again, spinning in the darkness, beneath the drop of blue. *Chatterley. You've erased. Erase the spent puppets.* Then bang, consciousness, like a new, burning little universe. The consciousness expanded. I sat up again. Dazed. *Hello.* In the little universe I felt the word enter my mind. Enter, as in enter with ability, leave a trace, an inkling. *Hello.* I heard an aircraft motor buzzing above me. The Piper Cub was back, the first son's model airplane. Was it flying on its own? Of course not. The boy. I made no attempt to reply.

The mortar round had struck the laser targeter, utterly destroying it. Clever trap. I stared at the pieces. Out of those fragments, what? The laser targeter had to have had a homing device, a signal emitter meant to bring that second shell into the designator. *One target, one kill.* The shell was like a bloodhound designed to find one convict. My designator. Smash the laser target designator. The assassination of the assassin. I cursed. The smart munition, an Einstein of death. The next generation will hone in on your heat, your light, your mental emanations, and designer viruses will be created to attack your own individual DNA. You'll have your existence and the virus will be your antigen, an antigen for your own genetics.

I realized I was staring at the shattered designator. Let the pieces of the targeter be found and the investigators make what conspiracy they could of the plastic and glass trash. *Okay, Mosley. It's finished.* I picked up my submachine gun and ran.

Three minutes later, as I fought through a tangle of brush and roses, my radio receiver cracked with static. The Somali depressing the mike button started to gabble in bad English, about the police car, the helicopter, the machine gun bullets shattering his windshield. The radio went dead. And I looked up. The Piper Cub model airplane swung in a wide arc across a meadow toward the two-lane road.

I reached the culvert and drainage system. The grate came off the pipe. I pulled the grate back over the hole as I entered the tunnel. The drainage duct was a meter in diameter. As I crouched I flipped down the night vision goggles—no reason to risk either a flashlight or a fall. Despite the dive into the ditch and the near miss of the mortar round the goggles worked. The tunnel makes several angled turns as it drops from the Mount Weather Complex. I had to move slowly. I realized I was stiff in my left shoulder. Perhaps I was bleeding. Yes, I was bleeding.

I left the tunnel. The patch of blood on my shoulder had spread. I went to where the trail motorbike had been stashed.

Michelle Malone, in her black leather bodyguard outfit, lay across the saddle of the bike, a bowie knife in her back. I rolled her body over. She fell in a heap.

I felt his presence.

I found him sitting beneath an oak tree.

Hey-Zeus Rodriguez had a bullet hole in his shoulder, a cigarette between his lips, and a crystal prism in his hand.

"I came here to cover your ass," Hey-Zeus said. "Your old pals Mosley and Garcia set this garbage up."

"Where's Garcia?"

"Dead. I killed him."

"How."

"Knife. His carcass is in the back of the van. Up in the mountains."

Chatt placed you. I placed the entire thought . . . without effort.

Hey-Zeus nodded, his eyes molten black. Then his eyebrows rose and his hawk nose bent as his Navajo cheeks tightened. "Yeah, she did," he said. "I have a certain subclass of abilities . . ."

"You can probe someone, to a degree."

"That's the jargon."

"You've got a feel for Mosley."

"According to the tests I'm a decent enough fit. Frightening, huh, to be a quiet man and to fit with an ego like that? When I was a kid I did a lot of peyote. Had little to do with religion and lots to do with my very local case of singularity." He tapped his skull. "Inside I can be as brilliant and as ditsy as Mosley."

"How did they find you?"

"They? The Shop? I was the grandson of one of the last practicing medicine men, a man who did it the old ways, none of the tourist tricks. There was this Bureau man on the reservation. Reservation, screw that ad campaign, on the concentration camp, amigo. And the Bureau man seemed to snap to the fact I was the grandson of Two-Eagle. Makes me wonder sometimes what my granddad was up to during World War Two. He was one of those Navajo radio men with the Marines in the Pacific, you know, one of the Code Talkers moving messages in encrypted Navajo that the Japanese couldn't decipher. I'll bet you know about that. Top secret in the big show of this century."

"I know about that. I guess I'm not surprised. The Shop has long roots. You said the guy who found you was a Bureau man."

"Bureau of Indian Affairs, not Federal Bureau of Investigation. Seems one of the standardized tests they gave us in the local grade school had a few of those hidden questions, the kind where the computers generate a profile that says you're able. Y'know what I mean by able. Shit. They sneak the questions into those standardized things, the whole battery of exams, using the old education testing service routine. You think you're answering questions about verbs and adjectives or what year Crazy Horse nailed Yellow Hair for the Forked-Tongue Sins of the Great White Father but they're looking for . . . for their weapons, man. That's how they glean us. Scholastic aptitude isn't what they're after."

Hey-Zeus shook his head derisively. "Well, The Shop tracked me, wolves to the stupid buffalo, kept track of me. And one day the Bureau man calls me in and says I have a new suit and a scholarship to George Mason University in Northern Virginny. A ticket off the concentration camp. Bingo. I'm a taker. You know The Shop's motto: *Destroy and Incorporate.* Now I'm . . . I'm part of the Great Process. Sensational, huh. Extrasensorial me." He smiled, then brought his hand up to his wounded shoulder. The smile faded.

"Why didn't Chatterley stick with you? Let you do Mosley? Why bring me in?"

"Why not have me kill Mosley? Is that really the mission? I don't know. Do you know? What fits? I used to worry about that, how all the pieces would get together, but now, like, I'm merely hanging around for the next sunrise. I'm just a soldier, man. The big picture. That's for her big mind."

I snatched the crystal from his hand and started to focus.

"No—she said no. Put it down," he said. His powerful hand grasped the diamond lens. "Later, man. You can settle what's what later with Chatterley. We gotta get the hell out of here. I got a bullet in me."

No. You don't get it.

"Man. I don't get what? And since when can you place thoughts? Shit truth on me. You that able? Are you? There you go again. Man, I *feel* that. That's totally weird placement. Don't spook me like that."

"It felt different than a probe?"

"Yeah . . . different than placement. Like you were pulsing brain. More than just the fuckin' idea."

We stared at each other. "I dunno," I said. "I don't know when I learned to place. It's been back there. I feel . . . I did it, didn't I. I'm doing it." I felt giddy. Christ, I felt powered. I'd popped a sentence right into his brain, easy, better than anything to date. But the power drained me. The focal energy sapped me, more than the wound in my shoulder, the wounds in my memory.

"What's that?" The toy Piper Cub came over the ridge. "Recon drone. Lez git." Hey-Zeus stood up, clutching his shoulder.

"Easy. This is what I was getting at. I'm sure the plane has a camera . . . but that camera won't be the problem."

The engine sputtered. The model airplane dived straight toward us. It crashed in the thick Virginia bush, its robot ailerons holding the stall, its wings snapping as it struck the trees.

Hardin Duncan, the ex–first son, came over the ridge on horseback. The boy was riding an Appaloosa. He had the airplane controls in his hand, a backpack on his back.

Hey-Zeus pointed his sub at the kid.

"Don't sweat it," I said, tapping the sub's barrel. The Navajo lowered the weapon.

"Hello," Hardin Duncan said.

Hello, I replied.

The boy smiled. Perfect placement. *Hello,* he replied.

Hey-Zeus Rodriguez's black eyes burned through the mental space between us. The Navajo muttered. What he muttered didn't matter. The man is quick. He understood. He had worked for The Shop long enough not to expect anything, not to reject anything, not to believe or disbelieve anything. He had the simple wisdom to react, take his next step, continue the mission no matter how improbable, how vicious and damned.

"I'm coming with you," Hardin said firmly. "I've no intention of going back. And I know who you are. You can't deny me this time, sir."

"We won't explore that now," I replied.

"You can't, mister—"

"Shut up."

"But my—"

"Both of you shut up," Rodriguez interrupted. He flung Michelle Malone's dumpy body across the back of Hardin's pony. "Talk your crazy talk later. We gotta beat it."

"She's in Wyoming," Hardin Duncan said, cocking his head at an odd angle, then pushing his glasses back up on the bridge of his nose. He shifted in the saddle, and grimaced as the dead body in black leather shifted with him. Hey-Zeus finished tying Malone's hands together beneath the belly of the horse. "Did you hear me, sir? Your daughter is in Wyoming . . . I also know who she is." His nod was solemn, resolute yet unaffected, a child's nod, a most usual nod.

I didn't ask him how he knew. Hardin Duncan was most certainly an able child, a young man of vast capability. Surely he could place, elicit, perhaps direct, or, when he matured, he would be able to do so. I smiled. Chatterley sure as hell didn't need a conspiracy of standardized tests or the aid of Navajo medicine men to cull Hardin from the teeming population. He, of all people, had been planned.

"My airplane. Please retrieve it."

"Now that's a silly bitch to carry. It's got a ten-foot wingspan," Hey-Zeus complained.

"No," I said, getting an inkling. "No. That's a good idea. Let's take it."

I rode the motorbike with a broken wing under my arm. On his bike Hey-Zeus hauled the fuselage.

Fourteen

H awkins," Hey-Zeus said.

"My real name is Wesley," I replied. I put the cup of coffee down on the dashboard of the van. I watched the windshield wipers slice at the hard mountain rain.

We had disabled the emitter on the van and stashed the trail bikes on the carrier on the roof. I had crushed my Mosley Synoptics message beeper beneath a tire, over a thousand miles ago. I had picked up every fragment of the beeper. The fragments had been, ultimately, thrown into the Mississippi River as we crossed it. (Hey-Zeus simply put a bullet through his and pitched it into a bush, along with his bloody shirt.) The planet-wide person-hunt—well, we had evaded everything, from street cop to satellite. My abilities, the kid's, Hey-Zeus's, even without a prism, without resorting to Prism—without contacting *her*—they gave us great anticipation. And Hardin Duncan said he knew Courtney was still there. She was okay. That tracked, Hey-Zeus observed, because Mosley certainly knows how to keep a hostage.

Sure, the West Virginia cops found Michelle Malone's body. But the official story identified her as a young California woman missing for ten years, a drug-head and a whore. No connection at all to Mosley, not at all. And the smiling black-and-white glossy shown on CNN was, no doubt, that of Michelle ten years ago, as an overweight flower child, the round face surrounded by long hair, not leveled with a punk flattop. Like that, ten years of Michelle Malone's life in The Area erased. The black-and-white glossy on the video screen dissolved into a lump of black leather found in a hole in Virginia. Nothing was ever said about Bullet Garcia's body. They had to have found it. But that's the usual. When Green Berets die they never say anything, for reasons of national security, and you know what national security means. Nothing was ever said about Malone's and Garcia's message beepers. And of course they found Hardin Duncan's Appaloosa, discovered as it drank from a tributary of the Shenandoah River. The authorities, given the presidential assassination, were scouring the Virginia and West Virginia countryside, concerned with kidnapping but also operating on the theory that the young Duncan— distraught by his father's violent murder—may have been thrown and might be dead in a briar thicket or along a West Virginia country road.

As for the assassins of President Duncan, the Somalis in the pickup truck and the man killed by the UAV took that rap. Yes, a rumor running around Washington had it that smashed parts of a second laser targeter had been found *on the other side* of the meadow. A "second laser" conspiracy theory, right out of JFK and Dallas and Lee Harvey Oswald

Land, was already making the circuit. There may have been a fourth Somali. The killing chaos of Mogadishu had reached Washington, penetrated Virginia. Should the U.S. invade Somalia as reprisal? What about the role of the U.N.? PBS aired a special entitled "Cold War with the Third World."

Coleman Mosley was on every talk show. Larry King explored the issues. The air attacks on Said Farah Hassan's home clan village were live through the low-light filter of the Cable News camera on board a hovering Apache helicopter.

Carolyn Duncan—her agony was perfect. On the TV monitor in the van we watched the process. She wore the black velvet dress and black mink stole, the black net scarcely shielding the round face with the black-lensed sunglasses, lenses like dark prisms.

"Okay. You're Wesley," Hey-Zeus huffed. He moved his bandaged shoulder with discomfort. The wound had been clean. No need for sutures—the cold dressing and the shot of antibiotics did the trick. "Okay, I keep forgetting. I used to know Hawkins. But who the hell you are and who I am pales when it comes to calories. The kid's hungry and so am I. And I know it's going to be another long and fretful night."

We ate in a diner south of Cody. The place has fifty elk heads on the log walls and thirty bear rugs on the bare rock floor. There's a drum in a glass case. The brass plate above the case says the drum belonged to Sitting Bull. And there are a half dozen TV sets, all attached to the satellite dish.

On the TV monitor above the counter we watched the procession across the Memorial Bridge, as recorded by the pool camera for CNN. The empty caisson clattered on the bridge stone, the horse-drawn carriage with the casket moved with measured pain. Hey-Zeus went to the jukebox. He dropped in a chain of quarters. The first song on the jukebox was the one I'd heard in Northern Ireland, the one about CNN and New World Orders. *The dogs are trained to handle violence, the machine guns are all greased and silenced.* More lyrics, then a piano interlude, then: *The culcha clowns remain concerned with the lifestyles of the richest worms, talk shows repeat global has-beens, sound bites pass for gospel wisdom, we got the Senate for a power base, we got commandos just in case, so don't bug out if the vic'try's Pyrrhic, we got ten billion stashed in Zurich.*

The next four or five tunes were Motown standards.

The ex–first son chowed down on cheeseburgers and chocolate cream pie. He didn't pay much attention to the burial ceremonies on the tube or the tunes on the jukebox. I bought a map in the curio shop. Hey-Zeus bought a new bowie knife. He said he liked the heft of the handle.

"I'm not going back to my mother," Hardin Duncan said as we drove further south, the mountains getting higher, the rain that much harder.

"That's the thousandth time you've said that," Hey-Zeus replied. "You think if you talk it enough it won't happen? Half the earth's looking for you."

"That's a scam," the kid shot back.

"Hah. You're hot potatoes. Bet they send out some of the newbies to look for you, the neural-digital interface troops," Hey-Zeus said, raising an eyebrow.

Hardin replied with a bored scowl. "So what if biocomputing and cutting-edge neurology allow neurons to be integrated directly into silicon chips? So what if integrated circuits can be embedded directly in an un-able brain's neural structure? You think it's a big secret those items are going into the brains of selected special operations soldiers? Well, do you, sir?"

"No," Hey-Zeus grinned, his wide eyes amused. "But it is interesting. I mean, the un-able suddenly communicating brain to brain psychodigitally."

"I'd say it's half-assed, that's what it is, the sorry best the technologists and mech-heads can manage," Hardin said. "So what if these biochips allow brain input and output to bypass sensory organs and go directly to the cognitive centers? They're only fifty thousand years behind, in evolutionary terms. Even my mother says that."

"I dunno," Hey-Zeus said with a baiting wink. "The techno-troopies are talking brain to brain, using those chips."

"But where's the technology, sir, where? It's not needed in The Shop." Hardin's voice rose. "The Shop doesn't need the gadgets. The gadgets don't give the un-able one percent of your mental gifts, much less what my mother and I possess. The gadgets have no psychic power in the least, not an iota, sir. The Shop only needs to be able to use these gadgets and knickknacks, to give the un-able the means of responding more quickly to a command." Hardin raised his own eyebrows. "The brain cells on those circuits, sir, those being placed surgically in the soldiers' brains. My mother chose those cells."

"She did, huh?" Hey-Zeus winked at me, reached over and flipped on the van's TV set. The latest half hour iteration of Headline News came on with a blast. The CNN newscast covered the presidential funeral and also the case of the missing ex–first boy. "See that? You're news every twenty minutes. Don't tell me you're not worth a maximum effort."

"It's a scam," Hardin said as he opened a bag of potato chips. "It is all a scam, sir. Ask Wesley . . . it's a scam, isn't it, Wes?"

I looked at Hey-Zeus. No, I didn't place the thought in his mind. He's swift. But no he wasn't quite getting it.

"You mean there are other ways to find you. I understand that," Hey-Zeus said.

"No. He means if his mother wanted to find him she could."

The Navajo cocked an eyebrow.

We left the road. I put the van in four-wheel. We left the jeep track and crossed bare rock.

We camped in a wood line. Inside the back of the van—a van hauling its own micro machine and electronics shop as well as enough sophisticated weaponry to take down a city the size of Reno—back there the kid finished reworking the Piper Cub's wing. Hey-Zeus and I took the trail bikes down from the carrier on the roof. As the rain stopped he took the wing from the van and mated it to the fuselage. He ran a systems check. The camera in the model airplane worked perfectly.

"It really is a recon drone," Hey-Zeus said.

"Yeah. Homemade," Hardin replied. "To hell with Lockheed Martin, Boeing, and Israeli Aircraft Industries."

We watched the news the next morning. Hardin Duncan was working on the Piper Cub's engine, testing the propeller. Hey-Zeus and I ate bran flakes and yogurt.

The now ex–first lady was being sworn in as vice president of the United States.

Hey-Zeus put his bowl down on the ground. He shook his head. "Are you surprised?" Hardin asked. Hey-Zeus said he was no longer surprised by anything. Two minutes later Coleman Mosley was appointed secretary of the treasury. Former vice president Masterson, now the president, gave a short, solemn speech. Carolyn Duncan stood next to President Masterson. She smiled. The new president smiled. She waved. He waved. She cried. He cried.

Hey-Zeus pointed out the doubling. "See the pattern," he said. "Dammit. I see it."

"If you'd use a prism you'll confirm your suspicion," Hardin said.

"You know how to use a prism, Hardin?" Hey-Zeus asked with irritation.

"She can double through him, through Masterson.

She couldn't through Duncan. The guy could resist my mom. Masterson's a pushover."

"How do you know."

"That's the plan," Hardin shrugged.

"He knows about prisms," I said.

"Yeah. You know about prisms. But are you alive? You aren't too moved by your dad's demise," Hey-Zeus said. "You watch your mother and say harsh words."

Hardin scowled. "My father isn't dead. That guy Duncan was a scam. A front. You know, a dude in a suit."

The boy spoke it flat, without emotion, the utter matter-of-fact of a child for whom the world has no magic, no illusions, for whom the world is merely information and channels.

"She can't hide anything from me," the boy continued. "Well, she can if she has the energy. You, Wesley. Running you guys is nothing compared to contending with me, if I wanted to be contentious. Mom would have killed me a long time ago if she didn't love me. Or what she calls love."

Hardin Duncan shrugged and spun the propeller on the model aircraft engine.

Horror entered the Navajo's bony face. The realization moved slowly, brow, eyes, cheeks, the graying kind of incisive, momentary cancer.

Fifteen

From our perch in the rocks we could see the valley, the green avalanche of conifers, the open flank of alpine meadow, the ranch house, the ice-blue lake, the small round knob of the machine gun pillbox covering the hidden entrance to the tunnel. The stable house and horse corral, with armed guard wearing a black Stetson, sat on the knoll beyond and above the tunnel.

"We're fooling nobody," Hey-Zeus muttered. "They expect us."

I lowered the binoculars and nodded. "Yes."

Sure they expected us. But they did not know where we were or even who we were. No, we hadn't been probed. Not by Chatterley. We had not used Prism. She had not used Prism, either.

I rolled over on my side and added: "But they're worried. For a change they know zilch. And we won't be probed. Not by her."

Hey-Zeus bit into a yellow stalk of grass. "The kid blocks, doesn't he? He blocks her out. I don't know what he does but I sense it."

Yes. Hardin Duncan had extraordinary ability.

Hey-Zeus rolled the stalk in his mouth. His lean face tightened into angles. "He's like some sort of psychic countermeasure, isn't he?" the Navajo said with dry bitterness. For him the irony wasn't difficult, simply bitter. He was a victim of knowing. "Well? Am I wrong?"

"I suppose."

Hey-Zeus plucked the stalk from his mouth. "No, you don't suppose, Wes. You know. I know you know." The Navajo shrugged. Yes, he had abilities. "All of us can block her out for a while, hold to ourselves. You can do it. I can. But the kid does something else. Someday the sharpies will have a theory. They always find a theory because they're paid to find theories." Hey-Zeus sat up and crossed his legs. He looked down toward the ranch. But he wasn't finished. That's the pain of knowing: there is no physical or psychic quiet. You know when someone who is riled is not about to finish. "Invent the spear, invent the shield. Invent the machine gun, invent the tank. Don't you look away from me, Wes. *We* can't hide. C'mon, look at me. You know what I'm getting at. Measure and countermeasure—hey, the Great Process. Ballistic missiles, then ABMs. Then we had the electronics dudes with electronic warfare and electronic countermeasures. Now, mental warfare, the power of the extrasensory." His ironic smile was cruel to watch. He had the pain of knowing. He tapped his high forehead with his finger. "The Shop finds Chatterley. Ultimate weapon, right? Well, that's the idea, isn't it? But by damn she breeds, and the kid is her countermeasure. Hey babe, the next generation of weapons is right behind you, in diapers, crawling on its hands and knees. Try and laugh it off or try and kill it off. But you've ambition, ambition coiling in you. You wanna rule the world? Better get thee to a nunnery." The Navajo leered. It was not a pleasant leer. His look was complicated; the man himself was as complex as what he saw. His eyes hardened to black beads, the look you get when you've had an articulate glimpse of oblivion.

I didn't reply.

I raised the field glasses as the helicopter rose above the far ridge line.

A helicopter flew air cover for the ranch. The chopper stayed at medium altitude. Through the binoculars I saw a flare dispenser slung beneath the aircraft. You don't have to read minds. Mosley's guys knew Hey-Zeus's van had a couple of shoulder-fired antiaircraft missiles on board.

Sure Mosley expected us.

But even in a world of sensors, countless monitors, in a world waiting for your return, surprise can be achieved. When you know what your enemy knows.

We knew about the nerve gas canisters in the airlock behind the blast-door entrance to the tunnel. We knew about the nerve gas for two reasons: Hey-Zeus had helped lug the GB Sarin nonpersistent nerve gas canisters up to the ranch and Hardin had probed Courtney's mind. Through my daughter's eyes we knew the layout from her side, from the room with the phony log-cabin walls abutting the concrete sides of the tunnel complex. And Courtney knew where to look and what to look for. She had seen the airlock when they took her in, when they let her out. She had seen the metal canisters.

The defenders' idea: the canisters were to empty into the closed airlock, to seal the entrance should someone try to get in and to keep those inside from getting out.

Still I said we needed more intelligence.

So Hardin—after insisting he had the ability, after demonstrating the ability to enter a mind, after entering my mind, after entering the mind of Hey-Zeus—put the prism before his forehead, focused, and proceeded to probe the mind of the guard at the central command computer node. The guard was reviewing the computer file on the command-activated minefields. Through the eyes of the guard Hardin got a look at the minefields in the alpine meadow. Hardin also got much more. The kid could not filter for information. He caught the entire conscious moment of the man.

The guard—we'll call him XYZ, to depersonalize his death, Hardin said—XYZ was sulking. He thought himself a victim of Mosley. He did not care much for the Employer. He only cared about his paycheck, his next meal, getting through this shift, meeting a waitress up in Cody maybe sometime next week, a waitress with boobs. But there was a prob, man. XYZ had a hernia. He had a kid by his ex–best friend's ex-wife, a kid he'd never seen except on videotape. XYZ had flunked his state trooper's test in Missouri and that was a week before his mother died of some bone disease they get in Kansas City. XYZ—well, he has to be depersonalized so the killing can be easy, Hardin argued. Otherwise, the more I know the less I can stomach his death, Hardin said. Yes, the conspiracy of knowledge, of knowing the good and the bad and the banal of a fellow human being, affected Hardin. Knowledge crushed the killer inside him.

Until XYZ—was it daydream or nightmare?—until the thought crossed XYZ's mind that maybe that twelve-year-old dolly in there in that big room was woman enough for a twenty-five-year old herniated hunk of man like . . . like Archie. Like Archie Earle. XYZ? I'm Archie Earle. "Maybe," Archie Earle thought, with Hardin entering the thought, but not the emotion, "maybe that hostage dolly in that room thinks I'm cute and maybe a young thing like her, with a hunk like me, it might be—"

Hardin's probe snapped. It stopped cold.

He was frightened. And with fear his ability to focus decreased.

"You can kill him," Hardin said.

"Now XYZ deserves to die?" I asked.

Hardin nodded. The boy's face was white as a sheet.

"There are things you don't want to know," I said softly. "Or you won't be able."

"I know you have affection for my mother," Hardin replied. His voice was also soft. "And once she's had you she won't let you quit."

The night was bitter cold. Fall night in the high mountains has all the sharpness of winter. We stayed beneath our heat cloaks, occasionally peering out through the narrow vent. In the cold night air our breath condensed like short-lived ghosts or the last weak dissipation of an evil dream that no longer holds its shape. Beneath the cloak I boiled water in the pressure chamber and mixed an egg and bacon MRE, the freeze-dried meal-ready-to-eat. Hardin munched an apple. Hey-Zeus sipped on coffee. Hardin threw the core into the gray rocks. I peered into the night through ambient-light-amplification goggles, into the emerald green amplified night where the hard diamond stars are hazy, green, alien suns.

We had the layout of the ranch. We had our weapons. The ignorant, the Luddite would call them magic.

Hardin had his ability. The technologists in the narrow paradigms of mathematics, electricity, silicon, and metallurgy would call his ability magic or quackery. A shaman in an Ice Age cave would have called it his magic, had he peered into a facet of the clear cut stone, had he found a channel, had his abilities, his powers, suddenly magnified and flourished in that channel. For Hardin Duncan, spying out the tunnel would be spelunking in the New Age cave of the mind. Weird, but it works. It is. And because it is, because the powers are there, they become weapons.

Yet anyone unfamiliar with electronics, heat-imaging, night vision devices, and their countermeasures (say, an interloper from the nineteenth century, an interloper arriving before time becomes a weapon of politics, before our evil perfects a means of changing history by intervening in history, by devastating and redirecting the past as it happens rather than merely burning books or putting words under erasure), such an interloper would have called our other weapons magic, the firesticks and conjures of demons or the carnival fakery of a weapons-crazy Oz trying to delude. But the weapons exist. And I used them. I used a laser dazzler to confuse the two essential visual sensors covering the path down the cliff. The heat-radiant garment—a cloak releasing a nonhuman heat signature—I wore registered to the body temperature of a fat bear getting ready for hibernation. And with the acoustic pads on my shoes I would convince all but the most astute guard at the central defense computer console that I was an animal, an animal other than human. And XYZ— Archie Earle—was not so astute.

I shot the guard standing beside the corral with a silenced nine-millimeter round. The bullet slapped from the MP5's baffle and hit him in the head, knocking him to the frozen muck. I heard the horses shuffling, breathing. For a moment my heart raced like wild cattle, raced eerily. I felt an inkling—a probe?

Chatterley—damn you.

I felt like air.

Chatterley!

The sensation passed. Hardin did his thing.

I low-crawled across the meadow, avoiding the half dozen claymore mines. I crawled back up the ridge to the air duct. I wrapped the plastic explosive around the bottom of the air duct. I tied off my rappelling line. I put on my gas mask and made certain the fit was tight. I waited.

* * *

A Piper Cub model airplane is not designed to be a cruise missile. Low tech with the right electronics, like a prism with the right mind, can suddenly blossom. Put the micro-TV camera in the nose of the plane. Stick a detonator on a wire protruding from the front of the engine. Pack the model airplane with five pounds of VDX and shape the charge for penetration. Yes, the model will carry it. It is now no longer a model: it is a weapon. String a trailing fiber-optic line from the aircraft (so that it spools out as the plane flies, reducing your electronic emissions signature since the guidance is no longer by radio) and tie the fiber-optic line to a sophisticated control device—a microcomputer with TV screen and toggle stick—and the model plane becomes a very smart weapon, a fiber-optic-guided bomb capable of striking with extraordinary accuracy. High-tech killing has returned to the hobbyist. The technological edge is back in your own garage.

The micro-TV camera on board the highly modified model plane had a low-light lens. Hardin had muffled the engine to where the once-raucous purr of the toy was now a whisper lost in the rustle of the aspens. Hey-Zeus took his position up on the hill. Hardin launched his homemade cruise missile. It rose, turned, its fiber-optic control line invisible in the darkness. The camera in the plane clicked on. Hey-Zeus saw the rocky top of the ridge—a greenish moonscape in the eye of the low-light filter. He pressed the toggle stick forward. The silent toy began its long glide over the firs and pines, the open meadow. Hey-Zeus saw the ranch house as clear as day, he caught the fence line. He flew the single-engine homemade missile straight into the vision aperture of the machine gun bunker in the meadow. The television screen blanked as the bomb smacked the narrow pane of armored glass.

The squat concrete pillbox erupted.

I heard the explosion, counted to three, and triggered the explosive packed around the air duct. The armored top of the duct blew upward like a flat disc missile. I scrabbled to the hole, playing out my rappelling line, and fired an armor-piercing grenade straight down the duct. At the instant the grenade hit the plate below, the duct exploded, and I fired a second grenade, a tear gas grenade, then leaped into the shaft. In one bound I fell forty feet, my boots slamming the smashed metal plate, the second bound taking me to the concrete floor. I turned one corner and fired three bullets into XYZ. Mr. Archie Earle crumpled. I fired a burst into the computer.

The lights in the tunnel complex were blinking and an electric siren wailed. *Dad,* she placed so purely. I turned into another hallway, found the doorway. *Get down, Courtney*—yes, I placed the thought, I more than placed, I directed her most-ably. *She hit the floor.* I sprayed the lock with a salvo of nine-millimeter.

I kicked the door open and tossed Courtney, as she sprang to her feet, a gas mask and a pair of gloves. My daughter is disciplined, and she knew what to do. She drew on the mask and got a tight snug fit as I fired another grenade down the hallway and killed a confused-looking guard.

"Are we going now, Daddy?" she asked. "You obviously know about the gas trap."

"Yes."

"Mosley's eldest son is here. He has an apartment at the end of the tunnel."

"Is he sensible?"

"Not in the least."

"So he doesn't have an escape route."

"I don't know, Daddy. I doubt it."

"Let's find out."

I blew open the door to Mosley Junior's apartment. Junior fired a blast from his poised shotgun and hit door frame, nothing, then concrete, the pellets chipping the wall behind me. I came up on a knee and put a burst into the heir.

I entered the room and saw him, or at least his image: Coleman Oswald Mosley on television, on a VTEL video-telephone linked to a high-density monitor. Mosley Senior's video image, his portrayal in the pixels of the monitor, was as palpable, as warm and cold as his reality.

Coleman Mosley watched me, or at least my image, from the distance of the television monitor, from its protective cage. There he was, staring, live on his own personal two-way CNN.

"What did you just do?" he screamed in horror, at the beetle-eyed low-light monster with the reptilian gas mask and silenced submachine gun.

"I shot your son and killed your son after he fired at me, live, on television, Coleman," I replied, my voice muffled by the speaker on the gas mask.

The moment, the agonizing moment: I watched the artery rise at his temple, on his forehead, live and in color, arteries and veins like the legs of a spider crawling beneath his skin, crawling into his brain, veins, moving crablike, now like a discolored net as the billionaire's eyes hardened, glazed, and the stroke forever froze the screaming Napoleon in his mind.

It was predictable, always predictable, like the endgame of a chess match between a grand master and a beginner, as the end of the conspiring nightmare is a cold sweat, fatigue, and the fearful moment when your wide eyes open and you discover you never slept one second.

There was the inkling, *the inkling,* like a cool edge of dawn, the cool edge of the approaching sword, *the first terror of knowing,* knowing that behind the line of icy dawn is potent nuclear fire. And my mind began to feel the pressure—somewhere in the tangled moments of clearing the tunnel complex and blowing our way through the nerve-gas chamber, of crossing the meadow, of stripping off the gas masks and coughing, of jamming an atropine nerve-agent-antidote needle into my leg when I realized I was having a reaction, of watching for a reaction in Courtney (she had none), of screaming to Hey-Zeus to fire the surface-to-air missile as the helicopter with its low-slung electric Gatling popped over the mountain and began to strafe us—and the Navajo turned, superelevated the shoulder weapon, and pulled the trigger; the launcher lurched and the missile ripped up the mountain in a swirl of fire and contrail. The Mosley Synoptics helicopter erupted in a greasy orange and white flash and fell blazing into the conifers.

Somewhere in that tangle of effort and event I felt her damning psychic pressure. I could not visualize the completion, I only saw the carnage. Destruction, Incorporation—the terrifying image of the blood vessels on Mosley's skull—and then my name, my name in my mind as real as an object:

Wesley.

"Hardin," I shouted. "Son. Dammit. Block—"

My voice stopped.

Hardin Duncan shook his head, his chin drooped, his glasses fell down his nose.

"Prism. It's a Prism contact," Hey-Zeus muttered. He threw the empty missile launcher onto the rock. He fell to his knees like a weird pagan worshiper, Ice Age and New Age—a worshiper I say I will never be. I looked again. Yes, he was on his knees. But forget the religion. The only religion recognized was power. Hey-Zeus responded with discipline, like a soldier committed to the might of his commander. "The kid can't do. He can't. He never could. Get that straight. She's contacting you, man. Respond. Dammit, respond. Get it done. So we can get the hell out of here."

I felt a pulse of energy. There was no fear, simply anticipation. I knew. I knew without and within the process. Mission finished. *Mission complete.*

But there was more. There was no release. She had to make her own dig, to use the claw. She had to let me know she has me, has had me, to let me know that my rebellion has been part of the small territory of living Hell she allows me, the acre of Hell where I think I am free to choose though there is no choice, only her plan, her objective, her ends achieved by my immoral means. Yes, there was more. Chatterley had to let me know I must answer. She had to order me to face her, face her on her terms.

She tried.

I resisted. *I fucking rebelled and made it stick.*

They felt it, all of them.

Go to hell.

The shake was small. Who knows what she felt. Who knows what processes I snapped, what wicked pulse from the last shallows of a decayed soul. I was sickened by the blood, the destruction, sickened by my complicity, my companions. The shake was small, a vibration. Perhaps all it takes to shake the universe is that kind of shake, the frail tear in the fabric, the microcrack in the foundation stone which spreads, turning concrete to dust, the spreading break like fingers opening from a long balled fist, prepared to release—

Don't.

It was plaintive, the voice, so damnable plain.

I paused. It was one of those moments when you simply decide. I stopped. I quit—yes, I am their creature. They know me. She knows me, dammit, she knows . . .

All right, Chatterley.

I pulled the hot, appealing crystal from my pocket and stared—stared so willing and so able—into its reflective, absorbing, too brilliant universe.

Sixteen

She made arrangements. I met her at Camp David, in the rough hills of Maryland.

"You must return my son," Chatterley said. And, for this moment, she was Chatterley, and for the moment, I adored her. "And you, Wes, are too valuable to lose."

"Hardin says he wants to go with me."

"Go where?"

"He wants to stay with his sister."

"You didn't answer my question. Where will you go?"

"Hell if I know." I leaned forward, putting my lips to her ear. "It seems you or Mosley torched my house." I leaned back.

Chatterley didn't reply. There was a wall. I didn't even try to enter her thoughts.

I looked at her bright eyes. Yes, she sparkled. She looked dramatic. And she had the look, the sex appeal of power. The Shop must have its hands on the controls of power. But it had never moved so overtly. No, I didn't say that right. Its control had never been so open. Here she was, Madam Vice President. If Hey-Zeus was correct, Chatterley could double through President Masterson.

"Why?" I asked.

She did not reply.

So I kissed her on the cheek, as I do when I return to her from whatever mission or oddball odyssey she assigns.

And she began to explain, in words, in thoughts, with velvet and steel, and there was a flood of explanation, a flood I could not absorb. I am certain she desired that effect. She could argue she gave me the truth, the total details, the full disclosure, that nothing had been denied. She could say there had been no conspiracy to deny information. And I would reply the density of information itself was a conspiracy, the inundation of knowledge is the best camouflage. How could I, a soldier, the sting on the tentacle, possibly comprehend the mass of knowledge, her detailed explanations?

Oh, I got bits and pieces, I caught stunning details, nuts-and-bolts specifics, but by and large I caught impressions as you catch them in the rapt flood of a dream. Sari (yes, I started when I heard her name, and Chatt saw the weakness)—Sari, Chatt said, had gone back to her emir. There had been an arrangement. An arrangement? I tried to halt the flood of explanation, to fix on the arrangement. Chatt waved me off, saying, "Did you ever think she might have been there to expose you?" but as I objected Chatt hushed me. She continued with the explanations, the details, the endless details. As the flood progressed I decided I would have to satisfy myself with impressions and the few details of "Why?" that managed to lodge.

"Why Mosley?" I demanded.

Her glance was complex, a nuanced sneer full of the joy of knowledge. Of course Mosley was a threat, she said. Money and anger are threats, but combined they are threats writ large, surely you recognize that? With the martyred Mosley (yes, he was already a martyr) made secretary of the treasury—even for the few short days he held the office—the angry members of Wake Up Planet Earth! now owed her. I got that. But that was like a dotted *i,* a mere brush stroke. Mosley had to die because he was on the way to knowing, Chatt said. Mosley, through his contacts, with his money and anger, had gotten close to the truth.

"We had the press brand him a kook when he said there was a conspiracy to kill him, but he was no kook," Chatt said evenly. "Mosley was getting close, Wes." Then she moved on. And I lost her several times, but I did get the impressions. "The media, Wes. You have to be able to sit in front of the camera and be, Wes, be there in front of the camera in order to influence, in order to lead. Mosley had it, Wes. Television short-circuits the traditional control apparatus. Never deny change," Chatt said. "Deny change and we become our own enemy. The Soviets failed to accommodate change. They could destroy but they failed to incorporate. This is a moment which requires us to emerge from the background. You don't follow me? Look, Wes, today the leader must be seen, seen convivially. It would have been a mistake to remain where we were, strictly covert. Mosley moved in front of the cameras. One of us had to counter. Do you understand?"

I said I wasn't sure. I said I thought any appearance from behind the scenes was risky. The Shop out front? Perhaps it was time to quit . . .

Chatterley scowled. I felt her pressure. "Well, here's something you can understand. Mosley's Global Security Division, fighting niche wars for a price. We played it loose, to see if he could have been co-opted, but some of these conflicts, if they get solved we want to be the ones who appear to resolve them. To the apparent victors go the political spoils and influence. Other conflicts, well, you know we've an interest in keeping the pot boiling. Jobs, business, buying bread, and throwing circuses require cash." She shrugged.

As I consider my memories I realize I have loused it, not done her justice. Her explanations were much more thorough, much more detailed, much more penetrating and acute. And she was more dramatic. Her bee-stung lips made each word more dramatic.

She returned the kiss. She kissed me on the lips. She did not kiss like a widow. The kiss brought me in. And when the kiss ended she returned to Hardin, tried to return to the subject of Hardin.

I demurred. As I said, this was an endgame between the master and the beginner, between the most-able queen and an able pawn. But I am an able pawn and I am an angry pawn. I blasted her about Courtney. And Chatterley reacted, reacted with brilliance, brilliance beyond her usual brilliance, her blue eyes afire. "That was a mistake, dammit," Chatt interjected. "My powers aren't absolute. Dammit, everyone

seems to know that except you. That's why we have to
have the entire spectrum of tools. My psychic capabilities lapse. I never get things perfectly, never. No one
but you has ever believed I can go much beyond
insights." She giggled that attractive giggle. "You
know my detractors give me credit for power I do not
have and could never wield. The other commanders
wouldn't allow it. Max. You know what he's like." She
chuckled.

Max? I only knew of Max through Chatterley. She
invokes Max when she needs another, a reinforcement, an alternative authority. I started to say, no,
Chatterley, I do not know Max, I do not know what
he is like, I do not know if he actually exists. I started
to say I accept Max's presumed existence and that's
enough. I started to ask her if Max had her powers, if
Max had the full range of abilities, if Max could walk
the edges of the Universe and bend pliant minds. Or
is Max dead, cold a long-ass time, or simply retired,
on the rocking chair, out of the line of fire? *Retire
and the next thing you know you wonder how you
can go on . . . staying alive.* So I said nothing.
Because Chatterley continued to talk. She has such
ability. And she said: "The Shop encourages personal
and political compromise. The Shop requires it. You
know that. You do know that, Wes."

"I'm not sure what I know," I said angrily.

She gazed at me.

"I know you let him have my daughter in order to
bend me." I felt a terrible urge. My hand curled into a
fist I scarcely recognized.

She placed her hand on top of my fist. "Wes," she
said soothingly. Her touch lingered. "Wesley, you big

idiot. How was I to know that Barb Angleton had once been approached by Mosley. That your daughter, whom we know can explore your unguarded mind, would get chatty and tell Aunt Barb a little of what was up. Courtney chattered. Money talks. Mosley's money talked to Barb."

"The car accident."

"We were lucky. The accident happened. We got a break," Chatt said, her blue eyes intense.

"But the cover story."

"Which one?"

"Mosley's ranch. I understand the Somali plot to kill President Duncan hasn't fractured. That's still in place. But we left Mosley's ranch a mess."

Chatterley cocked a sexy eye. "I'm surprised. You must be one of the few out of the information matrix. Two days ago we tried to arrest several Cheyenne American Indian Movement ethnic radicals and a militant gang of communalist survivalists, the very ones who attacked Mosley's ranch. Fanaticism, dear Wes, whatever its origin and motive, must be dealt with."

I felt a cold stream enter my heart.

She laid it out in a collected, authoritative, news anchor voice: "Our arrest attempt, directed at the Cheyenne and survivalist compound where the radicals had taken refuge, turned into a small war, with the FBI and Bureau of Alcohol, Tobacco, and Firearms on our side and the Cheyenne and survivalists on the other. They died defending their mountain retreat. We had to use aircraft and armored vehicles. We tried to be humane but we weren't going to have another one of those less than charming standoffs. A fire started, a terrible fire. I think they started it themselves. Self-immolation, like the Vietnamese Buddhists."

"Self-immolation."

"Yes. The assault on their compound was covered live on television. Everyone saw it. They had a chance to give up. They did not. Our negotiators tried. We brought in the psychologists and," she said without a trace of sarcasm or irony, "we brought in a few psychics. Criminals of the left and right should never attack the secretary of the treasury's ranch."

"No. They shouldn't. Why did they."

"Terrorists thrive on headlines." Chatterley glanced at a fingernail. "Hey-Zeus did an excellent job of being seen during your operation. That gave us the Native American uprising peg. The news organizations were already onto it as a possibility, so we followed their lead. And you were so perfect—the videotape of you in the gas mask–flak jacket–gloves assault outfit, total survivalist armed nut. That didn't need any spin. The communalist angle was a cute touch. Time to build a few new enemies, don't you think? Left-wing types have had their play. Everyone knows the right-wingers are cretins, gabbing about machines controlling the weather." She shrugged. "So let fools believe in technology," she muttered. She scowled and once more glanced at her fingers.

"And this short war was covered live. As it happened."

"Yes," Chatt nodded. "Every major network anchor was there. The cameras don't lie, do they, my dear Wes Hardin? One's own eyes do not deceive." Her voice was firm, assured, commanding. She picked up a glass of chardonnay and took a sip.

Then she added: "The world witnessed the event as it occurred. So how could there be any taint of conspiracy?"

She smiled. She has that kind of power.

And she kissed me once again.

Seventeen

I placed the letter from my bank in Lugano down
on the divan and looked out over the chalet's wide
deck. You can see the glacier from here. At times, on
clear Swiss mornings, you can hear the ice crack like
an old, unsilenced rifle shooting at the sun. The sound
echoes in the valley.

They tell me the glacier is retreating. You can see
the rubble at the edge of the ice cliff, the moraines, the
odd stones tracking its path of withdrawal and disap-
pearance. A day ago they found another old body, the
thaw of a long-dead climber. This young man disappeared in the ice on October 8, 1912, the day before
the Montenegrins attacked the Ottoman Turk garrisons
in Albania and the First Balkan War began, the day
before the twentieth century officially turned into one
heinous war. The climber had a staff and compass and
a meal in his backpack. He reached the mountain sum-
mit on his own, the toothy edge of the gray granite
ridge below the white-capped peaks. On his way back
the climber slipped and fell, disappearing into a crack

in the ice. Yesterday, like a messenger out of a dream, out of a slow process, he reappeared in the creeping ice, a leg, an arm, the leather-jacketed torso, a face with an open, astonished mouth, chilled eyes of horror and anguish.

I touch my brow.

The date of the climber's death. A hard detail. The climber's body. Another one of those bothersome details that attach themselves, make the experience more troublesome. I am trying to flee from the details, dismiss the suggestions of people, elements of recognized conversations, the pornography of terror, weapons, and common brutality. My eyes are sealed tight. I am trying not to see a damned thing, I don't want to see one goddamned thing . . .

Through the binoculars I see the edge of the glacier, where the body appeared. I follow the stream through the rocks and drifts to the meadow. I can see Courtney. She and Sari are in the long Alpine meadow, beside the cold stream running from the foot of the glacier. They are . . . they are taking water samples. Yes, that's what they are doing. By damn, that's what they are doing. Courtney's science project from the American School in Lucerne. They're trying to assess comparative purity. I spin the focus on the binoculars. The technology magnifies her image. The long blue skirt hugs Sari's slender figure. Yes, the emir understands other arrangements. My retirement as an arrangement, a comparatively practical arrangement. Tighten the focus, like the sniper centering his target: Sari is looking at something in her hand, at the mirror in the compact in her hand. She arranges her hair and closes the compact, slipping it into her pocket. Now Sari is looking up toward me and she is waving. The cool wind moves her dress. She reaches for her coat and brushes lichen from the nylon sleeve.

What I'm seeing changes abruptly. Sari then no Sari, like changing channels, video surfing, alive then not. And that's disturbing—

I am glancing at the roof of the chalet. The satellite antenna is rotating, moving, readjusting as the earth moves, tracking the geosynchronous communications satellite. I can hear the hum of its servos as the antenna shifts then freezes on the orbiting object in the sky.

I feel the eye of the camera. I feel the eye. Surely the spy camera is in orbit. The lens in the camera from God focuses more tightly. The mountains, the valley and glacier, the chalet, the man (is it the assassin, the photo analyst asks?) sitting on the chaise lounge. Tighter, bring the focus tighter. We must know, we must maximize what we know. There's the bank statement. Check the zeros—Five million bucks. My five million. A cool detail that screams that this is no dream, that with this end there is no denial, that the events, the people, my participation, all of it has been too real.

We need you, Wesley.

Chatterley's voice. And now the tightening lens is on the phone, the code-decode phone linked to the computer, the computer linked to the satellite dish, linked to . . . to my commanders.

The lens shifts. *Through another telescopic sight my sleep.* The man's (the sleeping killer's) brow wrinkles above his sealed eyes. He coughs (or is it a yawn?). He rolls over. There's a teacup (is it mint tea, the assassin drinks mint tea, or is it black coffee, now cold?) beside the bed. The low hum is the television (that's the noise) left on all night, the endless chatter of the talking heads, network anchors, the endless political bickering, shades and shapes of people in the great pantomime of power, of information, the endless going through hell documented electronically.

Is the glacier retreating?

The glacier of the Cold War retreated, leaving a terrible landscape.

Now the man on the video monitor is talking. What the hell is he talking about? I strain to listen. Yeah, he's an expert. The guy's an expert. He's yammering about the Balkans, about Somalia, about China, about the latest Kennedy assassination conspiracy theory, about the latest cocktail party and Senate hearing in Washington. He's talking. There are advertisements. He's talking. The United Nations is talking. He's inside the tube, trapped in the glass, in the medium, cool in the hot medium, yet he's quitting. The penalty. Cut to black. There's a string of commercials. I'm straining—

Who can quit anymore, Wes?

I'm waiting. With my hand configured in a fist I recognize I'm waiting for the phone to ring. *There is the sensation of the last-second search, of the shoulder nestling in the rifle stock.* I keep hearing the incessant ring. I am afraid. I am afraid of the ring. I know I will answer. It will be one of those moments when I simply decide. I am afraid the ring will occur and I will wake up and know this is no dream. I fear the finish of this nightmare.

Is the glacier retreating?

The phone is ringing.

I don't have the slightest sense of anticipation, of her mental pressure.

You can't say no this time, Wes. I won't let you. No one can simply quit.

You do have that kind of power, Chatterley.

The next time, the next channel, the next damning inhuman horror—

"Wes."

Sari shook me.

I woke up.

Sari and Courtney stood beside me, on the deck of the chalet. Across the valley I saw the glacier.

"We're back," Sari said. "Looks like you fell asleep."

"Yes," I replied.

I entered the chalet. The white Italian marble floor had been an expensive purchase but there is money for that, money for marble, for clarets, for very private schools in Lucerne.

I went through the den into my office. Hell, yes, I had been asleep. I have been trying to sleep, to rest, but I sense the moment, like an avalanche suspended, the momentum gathered and primed in the instant before release. Will I ever sleep? I have been trying to escape this terrible *anticipation*. I feel it approaching, this awful sensation of beginning.

It is more than an inkling. I am feeling the pressure. It is more real than gravity.

I sit down at my desk. I am at the desk. Reflected in the mirror on my desk I see the face of a frightened man.

The code-decode phone begins to ring. The ring is far away, but I am very aware.

My hand grips the telephone. The object is in my weakening grip. I must decide. I wait for guidance. I begin to shake. I hear the fracturing ice of the retreating glacier, a snap in the stream, a crack like the shot of a distant rifle.

AUSTIN BAY has worked as an author, journalist, Army officer, professor, defense consultant, war-game designer, advertising consultant, and newspaper columnist. He is the international affairs columnist for the San Antonio Express News and has published four books and more than two hundred articles on topics ranging from professional sports to military and political affairs. He has a doctorate in English and comparative literature from Columbia University and lives with his wife and two daughters in Texas.